12/24

DOUBLE CROSS

1943. The British have discovered a Russian spy network operating from the neutral fortress of Switzerland. Ultra, the handpicked elite of British intelligence, have taken advantage of their knowledge to plant a German double agent there to pass on signals to the Russians. However this perfect double bluff seems doomed to fail when German High Command begins to suspect false play. They plant their own agent in Switzerland to investigate. Only one man has a chance of finding the agent and liquidating him before the secrets of Ultra are blown wide open ... one-armed Major Cain and his team of lethal killers.

DOUBLE CROSS

DOUBLE CROSS

by

Charles Whiting

Dales Large Print Books
Long Preston, North Yorkshire,
BD23 4ND, England.

British Library Cataloguing in Publication Data.

Whiting, Charles
    Double cross.

    A catalogue record of this book is
    available from the British Library

    ISBN   978-1-84262-570-5 pbk

First published in Great Britain in 1978
by Severn House Publishers

Published in Large Print 2008 by arrangement with
Eskdale Publishing

Dales Large Print is an imprint of Library Magna Books Ltd.

Printed and bound in Great Britain by
T.J. (International) Ltd., Cornwall, PL28 8RW

Dedicated to
DORA, LUCY, JIM AND OTHERS

'Five hundred years of democracy and what have they produced – a cuckoo clock!'

Graham Greene

'The game of espionage is too dirty for anyone but a gentleman.'

Admiral Canaris,
Head of German Intelligence, WWII.

ONE

The winter sky was a bright and crisp blue. In the morning light the ice-crusted track that led to the camp sparkled and long icicles hung from the rusting barbed wire.

'Dachau,' Pannwitz said unnecessarily as the big black Horch passed the black-clad sentries and drove under the arch with its mocking legend *'Work Makes Free'*.

Gestapo Mueller nodded. He had been to the concentration camp often enough before. Without interest his penetrating brown eyes, hooded by nervously twitching eyelids, took in the scene as the Horch drove slowly towards the commandant's office: the crematoria, their chimneys already smoking; the compounds with their endless rows of dark brown wooden barracks; the stork-legged guard towers; and the shaven-headed emaciated prisoners everywhere, in their striped, pyjama-like uniforms, dragging their wooden clogs across the rutted, frozen mud, as if they weighed a ton. Somewhere he could hear the sharp crack of a bull-whip and the muted sounds of a gagged prisoner.

The Horch came to a stop outside the *Kommandatura*. Pannwitz got out first and

13

opened the door for his chief. Mueller smiled to himself; Pannwitz was obviously still very grateful for the promotion he had received for his part in the *Red Orchestra* business. 'Thank you, Pannwitz,' he snapped in his thick Munich accent and mounted the steps to the administration block.

At the door, the two steel-helmeted guards in the black uniform of the Death's Head Formation, snapped to attention and turned their heads inwards as he entered, as if they were worked by wires. Gestapo Mueller raised a wide, massive hand with huge, square fingers. '*Heil Hitler,*' he said without much conviction and marched inside.

The assistant camp commandant was already waiting for him in the hall, dressed in his best tunic, complete with the Sports Medal in Bronze and War Service Cross, Third Class, and he was obviously nervous. It wasn't every day that one received a visit from the notorious head of the *Geheimstaatspolizei*.

They exchanged salutes and Mueller got down to business at once, as they marched down the corridor together, Pannwitz following at a respectful distance. 'You received Reich Leader Bormann's communication?' Mueller snapped.

'Yes, Group Leader,' the official answered. For a moment he was tempted to ask Mueller what it was all about – the whole

14

damned puzzling business. But then he thought better of it.

'All Yids?'

'Yes, Group Leader. All Yids as ordered.'

'Good,' Mueller answered in his usual laconic fashion. Unlike the average Party boss, he didn't believe in talking too much; one gave too much away, and if he had to make others talk – well, he usually allowed his big fists to start them off.

Hastily the official opened the door to the inspection room for him to pass through. The big hall smelled of stale sweat, urine, and fear, which no amount of Lysol could ever conceal.

'Blonde?' Mueller queried, automatically sitting down on the chair in the centre of the room without invitation and crossing his booted legs.

'Yes, naturally, Group Leader. Exactly as was ordered by Reich Leader Bormann. And all of them have blood relatives alive and in custody in the Reich or one of the occupied territories.'

'Excellent.' Gestapo Mueller waved one of his big killer's hands. 'All right. Don't waste time. Bring them in. Let the dog see the bone.'

Behind him Pannwitz giggled at the phrase. Mueller froze him with a quick glance of his cold, brown, hooded eyes. 'Excuse me, Group Leader,' Pannwitz said swiftly.

The *Kapo* was the ugliest woman Mueller had ever seen and probably the biggest too. She filled the door in her striped uniform, with the purple flash of the homosexual on the tunic, her cropped jet-black head almost touching the beam, a thin, wire-bound, dog-whip in her nicotine-stained paw.

'*Ach, du heiliger Strohsack!*' Pannwitz gasped at the sight. Mueller pretended not to be impressed by the lesbian. Ever since he had joined the Munich police in 1919, he had trained himself to be unshakeable. 'You have them?' he asked, his voice completely under control.

'Yes, Group Leader,' the lesbian answered in a deep, husky voice. 'Six of them.'

Gestapo Mueller crooked his finger at the *Kapo*. 'Let me see them.'

She cracked her whip and turning to one side, allowed the candidates to enter. Obviously the Camp had taken some trouble with them. They were all dressed in fashionable dresses which reached to just above their knees. They all wore Italian silk stockings and the latest platform heels; and their blonde hair was rolled up all around in the current style – the 'all-clear fashion', they called it in Berlin.

Mueller nodded his approval. At his side, the assistant commandant beamed and clapped his hands together - like a pansy

16

choir-leader, Mueller couldn't help thinking contemptuously – and said: 'All right, tell them to undress.' Again the gross lesbian cracked her dog-whip and passed on the order, adding a few words in guttural tongue, which Mueller took to be the same command in Polish.

Without hesitation the women began to peel off their dresses, while the three men watched them without interest. After four years of war and concentration camps, all of them had seen thousands of naked women of all ages and all nationalities. To the Gestapo men, female prisoners were just animals with whom one rutted like an animal, if one got the urge and a prisoner was within grabbing distance.

A few minutes later, they were all naked, their new finery placed carefully at their feet, most of them holding their arms across their breasts, as if hiding them retained some modesty. Mueller clicked his tongue in annoyance and the *Kapo*, instantly understanding, cracked her whip threateningly and growled: 'The gentlemen want to see yer tits. Put yer hands down at once, cows!'

The women did as ordered and Mueller surveyed the six Jewesses thoughtfully. Behind him Pannwitz said, 'Well, you can see which one is the real blonde now, can't you, Group Leader?' He indicated the tallest of the girls, standing in the middle of the line, shivering with cold and humiliation.

'Shut your dirty mouth, Pannwitz,' Mueller snapped. 'And let's get on with the selection, eh?'

'Of course, Group Leader. Of course!'

Swiftly they eliminated the woman on the right of the line. A long scar ran from her pubic hair to her stomach. She had obviously had a caesarean operation. She was dismissed by the lesbian and told to dress outside. After Pannwitz had ventured, 'Remember, sir, he's supposed to be a ti – excuse me, breast man,' two others were ordered to leave because their breasts weren't firm enough.

'It's rather remarkable that they've still got any breasts at all,' the official commented, as if he were talking about cows at some provincial live-stock show. 'They usually dry up altogether in here, you know.'

Gestapo Mueller ignored him. His hooded eyes were fixed on the tallest Jewess, the only true blonde as Pannwitz had pointed out. 'Get rid of the other two. I've seen enough. Tell that one – the big Yid – to come over here.'

Hurriedly the *Kapo* carried out his order and pushed the girl towards him.

Expertly Gestapo Mueller looked her up and down, noting the high tight breasts, the flat stomach, slim thighs and the long grace-

18

ful legs, which were muscular, as if she might have once been a dancer.

'German?' he asked.

She nodded. 'I was born in Berlin, Group Leader,' she answered in a whisper. Her voice was scared, but not too scared, Mueller told himself, and her accent was that of an educated woman.

'Turn around.'

She swung round gracefully, like someone who was conscious of her body, and had been trained to use it to its best advantage. The Gestapo Chief reached out a big hand and squeezed her left buttock hard. She started, but didn't cry out.

Mueller grunted his satisfaction and said to no one in particular, 'The Yid cow has good firm flesh.'

He sucked his teeth thoughtfully and took in her face. If he had not trained himself for years to spot a Yid – the flared nostrils, the strange splay-footed way they walked, their difficulty with the pronunciation of the letter 'r' – he would have taken her for a pure Aryan. She even had light blue eyes. That was to the good too, he told himself. Their man liked cool Nordic blondes; yet according to the dossier supplied by the *BUPO* man, he could only copulate with Yids.

'What's your name, Yid?'

The girl flushed slightly. 'Rosamund – Rosamund Hirsch,' she whispered.

'Put a Sarah on that,' Mueller snapped. 'You know the regulation, Yid.'

'*Sarah* Rosamund Hirsch,' the girl corrected herself. Since the passing of the 1938 Law, all Jewesses had been forced to add 'Sarah' to their given names.

'That's better.' Without looking round, he clicked his fingers impatiently at the assistant camp commandant, who was beaming again, with self-importance. 'Papers – give me her papers.'

'Is that cow the one you want, Group Leader?'

'It's obvious, isn't it?' Mueller barked. 'Quick, I haven't much time to brief myself.' He looked up at the pale blonde. 'You, Yid, get into your clothes at once. We leave in thirty minutes sharp!'

Outside the sharp crack of the bull-whip, followed by the muffled cries of another gagged prisoner had begun again. Now the day had really started at Dachau Concentration Camp.

TWO

Impatiently Mueller dialled the number Bormann had given him, '439', muttering the figures aloud as he did so. The road from Dachau to the Obersalzberg had been crowded with troop convoys and they had made poor time. In the *Hoheitsgebiet*, the area immediately around the Führer's own residence on the mountain, they had been stopped twice by SS patrols; and the road which wound itself up to the Eagle's Nest, on the top of the Kehlstein, through tunnels and hairpin bends, had been dangerously slick with ice. Now they were late and the Brown Mole (as everyone called Bormann behind his back), the second most important man in Germany in this year of 1943, did not like to be kept waiting.

'Come on, come on,' he muttered, tapping the marble wall with impatient fingers until the lift came sliding down the hundred metre shaft which linked the tunnel with the Eagle's Nest at the top of the Kehlstein; two thousand metres above the ground.

Pannwitz, holding the Jewess unnecessarily firmly as if she might attempt escape in this, the most strongly guarded area in the whole of Europe, gasped as the door opened noiselessly.

The interior was gilded, with a ventilator and piped-in soft music, its centre dominated by a great red-plush chair facing the antique Venetian mirror. 'More of Bormann's work,' Mueller explained hastily. 'The Führer sits on the chair when he comes up here, which isn't often.' He chuckled, pleased to be able to show off his knowledge. 'He's scared the cable might be cut or break!'

'The Führer's own chair!' Pannwitz breathed in awe, pushing the girl aside. 'Would you believe it?' He looked at the overstuffed red monster, as if in his mind's eye he could see Adolf Hitler enthroned on it, while the lift whisked him up to the Eagle's Nest.

Mueller pressed the button. A second later they were on their way to the little mountain-top tea house, which had cost the Reich thirty million marks to build and the lives of twenty-odd workmen. But then, Mueller told himself, they were only foreigners – their lives didn't matter.

Bormann was waiting for them in the 'tearoom' as he called it, his brown-booted legs placed on the great round table, facing the roaring log-fire. Behind him through the window, which looked out over Bavaria far below, Mueller could see that it was snowing. Bormann noticed neither the snow nor the tremendous view of the Alps; he was too busy munching at a sausage sandwich.

'From one of my own pigs,' he announced, waving at Mueller to take a seat.

'Heil Hitler,' Mueller said and reminded himself that the Brown Mole had started his career as a farmer and would always remain a farmer, whatever high position he reached in the state.

Hiding his feelings for the gross little man with thinning dark hair and heavy pugnacious jaw who looked like a boxer gone to seed – for the Brown Mole was a dangerous man to cross – Mueller took a seat carefully and waited for Bormann to finish his sandwich.

Behind him Pannwitz, still holding the girl's arm, waited to be acknowledged by the Reich Leader, the man who had Hitler's ear these days.

Finally Bormann finished. He belched pleasurably and swinging his brown boots off the table, indicated that Mueller should follow him to the window. He had still refused to acknowledge the presence of the girl and an acutely embarrassed Pannwitz. In his familiar way, he grabbed Mueller by his tunic and pulled him closer. 'All this week, Fallgiebel has been running a check on all radio signals leaving the Führer Headquarters,' he announced grimly. 'My own adjutants have kept similar watch on the teleprinter operators. In addition every courier leaving the HQ has been searched by the Bodyguard.'

'And?'

'Nothing! Although we found a rather nice selection of pornographic photographs in Colonel-General J– But I'd better not tell you his name.'

Mueller's face remained stony, revealing nothing. He didn't need to be told the name; he already knew it. Just as he knew the names and details of Bormann's own stable of mistresses, ranging from the teleprinter operator in his own HQ to the minor actress at the Dresden *Staatstheater*. 'It was what I expected, Reich Leader. We had the same result when we ran a radio check on the HQ of the Greater General Staff in the *Bendlerstrasse* in Berlin. Nothing!'

Bormann's face flushed angrily. 'But if they're not getting the information they're transmitting to the Ivans from those two sources, where in three devils' names are they getting it? There's a bloody traitor somewhere somewhere at the very top. But where? *Where*, I ask you?'

Mueller did not speak; he had nothing to say – it was a problem that had been occupying his mind full-time ever since they had discovered the new leak, and the code experts had revealed just how high the quality of the material being transmitted to Moscow really was.

Bormann controlled himself with difficulty. He jerked a dirty thumb over his shoulder. 'Is that the woman?'

'Yes, Reich Leader. She meets up to all the requirements outlined in your letter.'

'Excellent. Tell me a bit about her.

Swiftly Mueller rattled off the potted biography which he had had learnt from the details the Assistant Commandant had given him in the dossier. 'Born in Berlin in '20. Full Jew. Parents had a jeweller's shop in the Kudamm. When they were arrested, she went underground.'

'Underground?' Bormann's thick eyebrows shot upwards.

'Yes, she had trained to be an actress. So when we started to recruit for the front theatrès she volunteered. Since 1940, she has hardly spent a day in the Reich. At the front, the stubble-hoppers are so happy to see anything in skirts that all thought of the Racial Laws leave their wooden heads.'

Bormann was impressed. 'For a Yid, she certainly shows initiative.'

Grudgingly Mueller admitted it, and then carried on. 'In December 1942, a paymaster in the Fifth Army reported her to the local Gestapo. Apparently the man wanted to sleep with her and when she wouldn't, he started to look into her background. One

25

thing led to another and she was arrested and sent to Dachau.'

'Praiseworthy initiative on the part of the paymaster,' Bormann said solemnly. 'I wish we had more folk comrades like that in Germany today.' He cleared his throat. 'What hold do we have over her?'

'Her mother is still alive in *Theresianstadt*. Her old man went up in smoke last year.' He made the gesture of spiralling upwards and snickered.

Bormann smiled, too. He knew well what Mueller meant; the old man had been put in the ovens. 'Good, good. Well, let's go and have a look at the Yiddish bitch.'

Self-importantly, the little man strode across the room with over-long strides and positioned himself, legs apart, pudgy hands on fat hips, every inch the German Aryan confronting an inferior, racially impure Jewish slave. He licked his dry lips. 'Open the front of your dress,' he commanded hoarsely. 'I want to see how much wood you've got in front of the door.'

The girl hesitated. Desperately her eyes flashed to the window behind him, as if for one wild moment she contemplated a suicidal leap through it onto the rocks far below. Bormann did not tolerate any resistance to his orders, especially from a woman and a Jewess to boot. He reached out, and seizing the thin material of her dress, ripped open the front. Her naked breasts jutted out, firm and high, thick-nippled. The girl fought back a sob.

'Excellent – *excellent!*' Bormann said in hoarse enthusiasm. 'Even if she is a Yid. That is the kind of bait we need for our man.' He took his greedy dark eyes from her breasts and gestured to her to cover herself up again.

He turned to Mueller again. 'She is exactly what we need for the mission, Mueller. She has all the physical and racial attributes. Obviously she can show initiative and as an actress knows how to play a role – the Yids have always been damned clever at that sort of thing. And most important, we have her in our power.' He clenched his pudgy fist triumphantly. 'She's the one. Now this is what you are going to do with her...'

Swiftly Bormann began to brief the Gestapo man, while the girl stood by numbly, her face blank of any emotion save despairing hopelessness. A Jew in National Socialist Germany in 1943 – what chance did she stand?

A MISSION IS PROPOSED

'The Russians are our superior in one field
only – espionage!'

Adolf Hitler, 1942

ONE

Major Cain changed down, and with the aid of his hook, swung the big camouflaged Humber staff car off the coastal road into the drive of the resort hotel, with its mock Tudor gables. He stopped the engine and patting his pocket to reassure himself that his automatic was still there – one could never be too sure even in the UK – he got out and immobilized the engine by removing the distributor head. It had been standard operating procedure on the coast ever since the big invasion scare of 1940.

For a moment he breathed in the icy sea air, listening to the growl of the waves below and the faint snap and crackle of blank ammunition from the bay where the Americans were practising beach landings for *the* day. Then with a little sigh, he crunched across the frozen snow into the hotel, its ground floor windows still heavily sandbagged and festooned with rusting barbed wire, from the days when the Army had evacuated all civilians from this stretch of the coast, and had moved in itself. The lobby with its plaster beams and imitation pewter was empty. Through the open door, he could see the dais in the 'residents' lounge', where he could visualize in peacetime a ladies' trio, playing sections from Ivor Novello to bored, comatosed guests. He shook his head in mock wonder. Zero C certainly did find some places to meet him. That last time they had met, it had been in a scruffy council 'semi' in a North London suburb; the time before that in a damp, echoing Scottish castle. Now it was this coastal horror.

Slowly he began to walk down the dark corridor that led from the lobby, lit only by a low-watt, blue-painted bulb, attracted by a radio, which was playing the inane jingle of that year:

'Mairzy Doats and Doazy Doats and liddle lamzy tivey,
A kiddley tivey too, wouldn't you?'...

He turned the corner and stood facing an open door. Inside the room, he could see the old-fashioned radiogram from which the music was coming. Suddenly he sensed that old feeling, that familiar, frightening sense of being watched, which three years of clandestine operations in Occupied Europe had bestowed on him, like a sixth sense. He spun round, automatic already in his hand, body half crouched and ready for action.

Zero C stood there, tall, hawklike, unsmiling.

Slowly Cain lowered his automatic and breathed out hard. 'It's not always wise to do that kind of thing in our business, sir,' he said.

'I know, Cain. Just testing your reaction.' He allowed himself a bleak smile, but his eyes remained cold. 'It's been four months since your last job.'

'You mean Ultra's on again?'

Zero C nodded. 'Now put that popgun away and let's go into the room. It's damnably cold in this corridor.' Cain stowed his automatic and smoothed his tunic with the flat of his gleaming steel hook. Silently he followed the head of the Ultra Organization into the little sitting room, heated by one miserable bar of an ancient electric fire.

'Take a pew,' Zero C said.

Cain sank into a scuffed leatherette armchair. Its springs protested under his weight. He reached out his hook towards the radio to turn it off, but Zero C shook his head.

'No, leave it on,' he commanded. 'One never knows.'

Cain did as he ordered, reflecting that even in the middle of the UK the MI6 man was as security-conscious as if he were in Occupied Europe on an Op.

On the radio, the Andrew Sisters began to recount the tale of the *'Boogie-Woogie Bugler Boy of Company B'* in shrill hectic harmony.

'Yanks!' Cain said.

'You know what the PM says, Cain,' Zero C answered, settling down in his chair and lighting a *Player's*, 'there is only one thing worse than having the Americans as allies, and that's not having them at all.'

Cain grinned slowly. 'I suppose you're right, sir.'

Zero C breathed out a stream of blue smoke pleasurably. 'How did you find the roads down here, Cain?' he asked, looking at the one-handed Major through narrowed eyes, as if he were seeing him for the very first time.

'Frankly, sir – *bloody!* I thought I'd never make it. You certainly pick them, sir.'

'We can never be too careful about Ultra. You know that, Cain.'

Major Cain did. He had been in clandestine operations in Occupied Europe for three years, but he had never really known what security was until he had joined Ultra, Britain's top-secret de-coding operation which could break any message sent by the German enigma coding machine. According to Zero C who headed the operation's security, apart from the boffins who actually did the decoding at Bletchley, there were only half a dozen people in the whole of the country who knew what was going on in Bletchley, all personally approved by the Prime Minister himself. Even Cain's own little team of specialists in murder and mayhem, did not know for whom they were really working. Churchill had even coined a new security priority for the whole op – *Ultra Secret.*

Zero C settled himself back in the cheap chair and fixed the Major squarely with his cold blue eyes. 'Cain,' he announced, 'I'm going to tell you something which is known only to C' – he meant the head of MI6 – 'myself and that crook, Colonel Dansey.'

Cain repressed a smile. He knew Zero C's intense dislike of C's deputy director, Dansey. In MI6 the old hands were all terribly power conscious, each trying to build up his private empire; and to Zero C's discomfort, Dansey was an empire-builder *par excellence.*

'In '40,' Zero C was saying, 'when Dansey was kicked out of Italy and that absurd Z Organization of his folded up, he took his crooked self to Switzerland and tried to justify his exorbitant salary by starting up a low-level operation against the Boche from there. Though God only knows what he expected to achieve from that place! In '41 the bugger somehow or other got on to the Ultra op. You know how the swine pokes his long nose into everybody else's business?' Zero C shouted.

Major Cain didn't, but he nodded encouragingly.

'It was just at the time when the Bletchley

35

boffins had begun to break the enigma messages indicating that the Boche were going to attack the Reds. Excuse me, these days we have to say "our Russian allies", though personally I still don't trust them as far as I can throw them.'

Cain did not say anything. He knew that the main enemy of the MI6 throughout the twenties and most of the thirties had been the Russians, and old hands like Zero C and his chief 'C' probably hated the 'reds', as they still thought of them, more than the Germans.

'Of course, the information put us in a bit of a fix,' Zero C carried on. 'How could we inform the Russians without compromising the whole Ultra op? In the end Dansey suggested that Churchill should send a special ambassador to warn Stalin personally that he had received information from one of our agents that the Germans were going to attack Russia. Churchill sent that sanctimonious parlour-pink Cripps, but Stalin only laughed in his miserable face and that was the end of that. Hitler caught the Russians with their knickers down!'

On the radio, a broad Yorkshire voice – one of the BBC's recent innovations to please the masses – was announcing *Workers' Playtime* to the accompaniment of hysterical female shrieking and catcalls. Idly Cain wondered why, in the middle of total war, the workers had to have a 'playtime'.

'Thereafter, of course, with the main Boche effort being made in Russia,' Zero C continued, 'Ultra started to pile up the intercepts about the Boche intentions there. Stalin would have given his eye-teeth for them. But how were we to get them to him without giving the game away, eh, Cain?'

'Yes, I see the problem.' He smiled. 'But knowing your devious ways, if I may say so, you found a solution.'

Zero C accepted the compliment with a slight nod. 'Everything was all right as long as the *Red Orchestra* was still operating.'

'You mean you had infiltrated the *Red Orchestra?*' Cain exclaimed in surprise. Everyone who, like himself, had worked on clandestine Ops in Occupied France had heard rumours of the tremendous Russian spy network, code-named the *Red Orchestra* by the Germans. It stretched from Berlin itself down to the smallest French provincial town.

'Yes,' Zero C answered airily, as if it were the most obvious thing in the world. 'We penetrated it in Brussels and Ostend and used our people in their organization to discreetly pass on what we had learnt from the Ultra Op. In 1942 when the Boche cottoned on, that means of transmitting information dried up. At this stage Dansey decided it was time he got into the act.'

'Through Switzerland?' Cain asked.

'Right. The Russians already had a reserve spy ring in that country. *Dora* it's called, run by a little Hungarian Jew, named Rado.' Zero C reached inside his pocket and brought out a photograph. 'This is the chap,' he said, handing it to Cain.

It was a hazy snapshot, obviously taken hastily, of a small, bespectacled man with the start of a paunch, who looked more like a professor than a professional spy. 'Doesn't look the type, sir,' Cain commented, giving the photograph back.

'He's not much of an agent, I agree, although he's been in the business for the Russians ever since they recruited him after the failure of the Bela Kun revolution in 1919 in Hungary. He's really more interested in cartography, which is his profession, and in his off-duty hours, girls; plenty of them.' Zero C smiled oddly, as if with pleasure at the other man's weaknesses. 'In short, the ideal man for Dansey and our Op.'

'You mean that we are going to infiltrate the – er – Russian *Dora* Ring?'

'Dansey has already done so. As soon as the *Red Orchestra* was broken up and *Dora* went into operation, Dansey began to use it as our main means of passing information to Moscow. Now up to 1942, Rado had been obtaining what bits and pieces of information he could, from travellers or German deserters who had crossed into Switzerland. He also had a couple of Swiss newspaper correspondents in Berlin, who passed him the odd item, and one of his agents was friendly with an officer in the Swiss High Command. But it didn't amount to much and by the time it got to Moscow, the stuff was usually out-of-date anyway.' Zero C sniffed disdainfully.

'But imagine old Rado's fix when Moscow informed him that he was in charge of the only Soviet ring still operating in Western Europe and that he'd better get his digit out of his orifice smartly and begin to produce. I should image he almost had kittens!'

Cain nodded. In the past, the Soviet Secret Service had not hesitated to assassinate its own agents who had failed and who were suspected of possible defection because of this. And the fact that the agent might be abroad did not stop the KKVD killers. In '39, they had even killed one of their own agents in the middle of Mayfair. A year later they had done the same thing in the heart of New York. Cain knew they were ruthless. For a moment he pitied Rado, but only for a moment.

'But where was he going to get that information?' Zero C was saying. 'Not from some runaway German squaddie or a fat-bellied Swiss commercial traveller to be sure.' He chuckled suddenly. 'But he had not reckoned with the Old Firm. In our usual charitable fashion, we decided to help him out. We put him in touch with Lucy.'

TWO

Cain waited patiently while Zero C lit another *Player's*. On the radio, the 'workers' were now indulging in community singing. *'Roll Out The Barrel'; 'Run Rabbit Run'.*

Zero C dropped the match into the ashtray. 'If you survive this war, which is hardly likely I suppose, and live to my age,' he announced, 'you'll probably read one day that Lucy was the greatest agent of World War Two.'

Cain didn't react. He knew that Zero C was provoking him by the oblique approach. All the spymasters used it with their subordinates. He supposed it gave them the feeling of omnipotence when they finally sprang their little surprise.

'Writers will probably make a fortune out of him and his brilliant coups, but then writers always do talk a lot of cock, don't they?'

Cain could restrain his curiosity not longer. Impatiently he rapped the point of his hook on the little side table and snapped,

'But who is Lucy, sir?'

By way of an answer, Zero C, obviously pleased to get a reaction from the younger man, produced another photograph from his inside pocket. 'Lucy,' he announced, handing it to Cain.

Cain stared down at the picture of a tall, bespectacled, sallow-faced man in a shabby raincoat and pre-war trilby. The man could have been of any nationality and of any poorly-paid profession. He looked completely undistinguished. 'There's your greatest spy of World War Two. Rudolph Roessler, Alias Lucy!'

'A German-Swiss?' Cain queried, judging the nationality from the name.

Zero C carefully stowed the photo away before he answered. 'No, *a German.*'

'What's he doing in Switzerland, sir. Is he a Jew? A refugee from the Jerries?'

Zero C seemed only to hear his first question. 'Lucy took up writing for newspapers after completely undistinguished service in the First World War. One year after the Nazis came to power, he slipped over the frontier into Switzerland and started up a small publishing firm in Lucerne, printing what I believe are called "advanced works".' He sniffed. 'You know, stuff by chaps like that Irish pornographer Joyce and his kind?'

Cain didn't know. He had not read a book, save a training manual or two, since the

41

outbreak of war. But he kept his silence.

'But Lucy could not quite forget his old Fatherland. He was always after German tourists, businessmen, and the like, passing through Switzerland, sounding them out about what was going on in Germany. And he was a great reader of all the German newspapers available in Lucerne's public library. You see, his firm wasn't going too well, which wouldn't surprise anybody who has ever attempted to read Joyce, pornography or no pornography, and our friend was forced to sell odd titbits of information – nothing worth a bag of beans – to anybody who wanted it. Naturally one of his customers was Colonel Dansey.' He smiled bitterly. 'How could it be otherwise? He was always a great one for wasting the taxpayers' money on nothing. That is how we became aware of Lucy's existence.'

'You mean that Lucy was – and is – the man who passes on the Ultra information to Rado and from him to Moscow?' Cain asked swiftly.

'Not exactly. We didn't want to make it as simple as that. You see, Lucy was to be our front.'

Zero C saw Cain's puzzled frown and said hastily, 'Look, you chaps out in the trenches, so to speak, always see things in blacks and whites. We in the Old Firm have to see them as greys. We can't do things as directly and straightforwardly as you young fellers can. This is what Dansey did. He knew that Lucy had already had some contact with Rado through an intermediary and that the intermediary had extracted a promise from Rado never to inquire about Lucy's identity. Naturally Rado kept his promise – he was only too happy to obtain whatever pathetic scraps of information he could get. Now Dansey took the thing a step further. Lucy was to take his information directly to the group's only operator for immediate transmission to Moscow so that no time was lost by letting Rado have it first. Naturally again, Rado agreed. What could be simpler for him? Soon Lucy's info started earning Rado all sorts of kudos from Moscow. He was awarded the Red Banner, third class, and that kind of enamelled junk with which the dictators always reward the dupes–'

'But where was Lucy getting his information from, sir?' Cain interrupted him impatiently.

Zero C smiled. 'He wasn't getting it anywhere. It was already there.'

'You mean the radio operator?'

'That's right. Alexander Foote, alias *"Jim"*, whom we'd infiltrated into the Ring back in '39, just in case it ever became important. He receives the information directly from Dansey in Berne. We get it through him in the diplomatic bag, or if it's really urgent by radio.'

'Exceedingly smart, sir,' Cain breathed, unable to repress his admiration of the devious ways of the Old Firm. Lazy, easy-going Rado, only too happy to receive kudos and not killers from Moscow, obviously would be completely satisfied by the arrangement, where the unknown agent Lucy, took his supposed information to the British plant, this man Foote. 'But how was Lucy supposed to receive his information from Germany, sir?' Cain persisted, knowing that Ultra was sometimes able to decipher Hitler's orders sent over the enigma coding machine, quicker than his generals in the field could.

'We invented a cover story for him,' Zero C answered. 'A quite absurd one, but it is remarkable what some people will believe. During the First World War, Lucy served in the German Army, as I have already said. There, according to our story, he made the acquaintance of ten officers. They remained in the service after the war and rose in their careers until five of them were generals. Today, according to the legend, eight of them work in one branch of the German High Command or other. Now, as convinced opponents of National Socialism, they all believe that Germany must lose the war in order to be rid of that man Hitler. Hence they are supplying Roessler, alias Lucy, with top secret info by means of the

German Army's own communications system, knowing that he will forward it to the Russians. It is as simple and as completely implausible as that.' He shrugged.

'But Rado believes it and so does Soviet Intelligence in Moscow. Why shouldn't they, Cain? After all, the information they are receiving does come from Hitler's HQ – *via Bletchley* – and it's absolutely top-notch.' He chuckled suddenly. 'Imagine what our writer chaps will make of those ten mythical officers after the war, eh? I'd like to see what kind of balderdash they will write, and of course they will. They always do, don't they, eh?' He chuckled again at the thought, then he was businesslike.

'But we think our nice neat little arrangement is going to run into trouble soon. Two days ago Bletchley picked up this.' He took a sheet of thin paper, with the word 'Ultra' stamped across its top in red, from his pocket. Cain recognized it immediately as one of the Ultra intercepts. In his shaky German, Zero C read out the message. '*Rote Drei in Betrieb – Sudwest Schweiz. Abhorstelle Stuttgart.*' [Red Three in operation southwest Switzerland. Listening post, Stuttgart.] 'You see they've picked up Foote's transmitter, and as the Boche have already broken the Russian code, it won't be long before they are aware of the high quality of the information being passed to Moscow.'

'But what do you expect the Jerries to do, sir?'

'The obvious thing would be to betray the whole network to the Swiss Federal Police. You know the Swiss? A terribly immoral nation of absolute stupidity on every subject save that franc of theirs – something to do with their five hundred years of democracy, I shouldn't be surprised. They'd do anything to save their pennies! So if the Boche tipped them off they'd collar the whole Ring as soon as you could say Jack Robinson.'

'But *you* don't think the Jerries will do that, sir?' Cain made it easier for him.

'No, for this reason. They will want to know who the traitor is in their own camp. Obviously he must be someone of high rank to have access to such high level information for the Russians and the Boche won't want a man like that to slip through their fingers, will they?'

Cain nodded his agreement. 'So?'

'So? They'll attempt to infiltrate an agent into the *Dora* Ring. It's standard operating procedure for an intelligence organization.'

'Yes, I agree.' Cain hesitated only a fraction of a second, as if it went against the grain to pose the question, yet knowing all the same that he must. 'And where does my unit fit into all this, sir?'

Zero C ignored his question. 'Now under ordinary circumstances,' he said, 'we'd simply withdraw our man and let the Boche get on with it. We couldn't risk them finding out what a pathetic agent Lucy really is and that the real source of Rado's information is not in Germany, but here in the UK – in Bletchley. If they did, Ultra would be finished! They'd alter their whole supposedly foolproof coding system and we'd be back where we were in 1940, as blind as a bat, without any clue to the Boche's military and political intentions.'

'But what are the special circumstances about this ring that makes you risk Ultra, sir?' Cain asked, irritated that Zero C was playing the spymaster again by not answering his other question.

'I'll tell you, Cain, and I don't have to say that the matter has been discussed at the very highest level. Winnie himself chaired the discussion. You see we must keep the Russians in the war until we and the Americans are ready to go back to France some time next year. But all this winter the Russians have been making irritating little noises. It sounds to the PM as if they are prepared to make a separate peace with the Boche if we don't help them soon. And you know how disastrous that would be?'

Cain nodded.

'Well, for weeks now, the boffins at Bletchley have been de-coding message after message from Hitler's HQ, ordering unit upon unit to the Central Front in Russia; in the area of Kursk. And you don't have to be told what that means, Cain, especially when I tell you most of the units are armoured and SS to boot.'

'A spring offensive?'

'Yes, that's our guess exactly. The Boche are obviously going to make one last major attempt to wrest back the strategic initiative from the Russians. Now it is imperative that we keep Lucy going until we have passed on all the information we have on the Boche's intentions. Then we can pull out and let the whole operation fold up. We'll probably inform the Swiss Federal Police about it ourselves – *discreetly* of course.'

Cain smiled a little at the cold-blooded calculation of the spymaster. They were all alike, 'C', Dansey, Zero C and the rest of the bosses. Once their agents had outlived their usefulness, they were dispensed with. For a moment Cain wondered what would be the fate of himself and his own men, when they were no longer needed. Then he dismissed the thought swiftly. It didn't do to dwell on such things. In the radio Big Ben was chiming out the hour, prior to the Home Service news. Zero C looked at his watch, suddenly aware of the time and began abruptly to hurry. 'Of course you'll fly out, Cain,' he said, buttoning up his shabby tweed jacket.

'Fly out – *where?*'

Zero C tapped his inside pocket to check whether the photographs and intercept were there. 'Where? Switzerland, of course. We've arranged for you to fly with the Clipper from Southampton to Lisbon. There you'll take the normal commercial flight to Madrid. In Madrid you'll take the weekly Spanish flight to Geneva. We'll fix you up with diplomatic passports, naturally.'

'Naturally,' Cain said ironically.

But irony was wasted on Zero C. Like all the spymasters he was completely without humour, unless it was of the sadistic kind. 'Any questions, Cain?' he snapped, rising to his feet and throwing a tattered, multi-coloured scarf around his neck. Cain recognized the colours of the Oxford college he had attended nearly a quarter of a century before.

Cain caught himself just in time. Zero C was using the oblique approach once again. He wouldn't let the tall, skinny spymaster rile him. 'Just one, sir,' he said, his voice quite calm. 'What is our mission?'

'Oh, didn't I tell you?' Zero C clicked his tongue in mock annoyance. 'Sorry. It's your job to find the Boche infiltrator.' He bent down and switched off the radio. Alvar Lidell's detached, upper-class voice died suddenly, and the room was very quiet.

'And then?'

'*Then?* Then, you'er – er to – what is the

word they're always using in those ghastly war films? You're to *liquidate* him!' He smiled coldly and strode to the door purposefully, as if a hundred more important things awaited him this cold February day. Abruptly he paused, as if something had just struck him. 'Oh, by the by, Cain.'

'Sir?'

'Remember, you'll be operating in a neutral country. If the Swiss police catch you afterwards, it will be regarded as murder. And naturally we would have to disassociate ourselves from you completely.'

'Naturally,' Cain echoed sourly. And with that the spymaster had gone, leaving him alone with his thoughts. They weren't very pleasant.

THREE

Ancient, tail-coated waiters shuffled back and forth bearing discreetly covered silver dishes. The lids hid thick, red château-briant steaks and braces of succulent part-ridges. Here, there was none of the usual austerity of the average London restaurant, with its whalemeat steaks, powdered egg omelettes, inevitably over-cooked Brussels sprouts, and a *plat du jour* which   t well turn out to be rissoles.

Most of the clientele was civilian: rich elderly ladies with purple permanents and rapacious, hungry eyes, and pompous 'important' men with mouths like rat traps and hard, threatening eyes. Here and there was a man in uniform, usually middle-aged with the red staff tabs on his collar, usually in the company of an awed pretty girl, who could well be half his age.

Colonel Hake-Smythe was no different from the rest, though well below middle-age. But his companion, Lady Patricia Gore, presently masquerading as a useful member of society as a leading seawomen in the Wrens ('I simply couldn't accept a commission, my dear. After all, that is what this war is about – *the people'*) was as pretty and silly as the rest of the young women present. Now she regarded her companion, with the dull-purple ribbon of the Victoria Cross on his chest, with admiring eyes, as he clicked his fingers at the waiter.

The old man shuffled across with the reckless abandon of a Home Guard with rheumatics. 'Colonel?' he quavered. Everybody in the black market restaurant knew how generous Colonel Hake-Smythe was with his tips.

'Another bottle of bubbly, George – and toot-sweet, what?'

'Right away, sir.'

The waiter creaked away and Hake-Smythe slid his hand under the table again and began to let his greedy fingers crawl up Lady Patricia's black-clad right leg once more. She giggled. 'Haven't you had enough of them yet, Colonel?' she asked.

'You know what they say about black stockings, Patricia? They're black on account of all the men who've gone over the top.'

The Colonel fumbled with the metal suspender and passed on.

Lady Patricia giggled again. Colonel Hake-Smythe's accent didn't sound quite right, but he was great fun. She had had a great time with him ever since he had picked her up outside White's the day before yesterday. He seemed to know everybody in town, had money to burn, and always knew places like this where there were none of those crude Yanks, who were always pinching one's bottom, and where the food was not so boringly plebeian.

The waiter came back and poured out the black market champagne. Colonel Hake-Smythe withdrew his hand reluctantly. He touched her glass with his. 'Bottoms up!' he called.

'What a quaint expression, Colonel. Where in earth did you ever pick it up?'

'The men – my chaps,' the Colonel answered and poured himself another glass of champagne. 'Terribly working class, but loyal, intensely loyal. And by the way, Patricia, don't call me Colonel. It sounds so terribly formal. Call me Reggie.'

'All right – Reggie. But of course, outside I'll still have to salute, you know.'

The Colonel chuckled wickedly and pressed her pretty black knee under the table. 'I'd much prefer that you saluted elsewhere – in bed, eh?'

Again she giggled; then she attempted to be businesslike.

'Now, Reggie, you know what the purpose of this dinner is? We've got to work out how we'll tackle Daddy about our engagement when we go down to our little place in the country this weekend on my forty-eight.'

Hake-Smythe's eyes twinkled with interest. The Gores' 'little place in the country' covered about half of Gloucestershire. 'Naturally, Patricia. Well, fire away, old girl.'

She pointed a finger at the medal ribbon. 'Your gong, for instance. I mean he'll be terribly impressed. He's very Army, you know. Local Home Guard commander and all that. But I'd rather like to know in advance what action you received it for. I don't want to appear too much of a ninny in Daddy's presence, as if I didn't know a thing about you – *oops!*' She gasped a little, as the Colonel's hand went a little further than it should have done in a public place. 'Reggie, remember the VC!'

Colonel Hake-Smythe withdrew his hand. His face creased into a frown. 'It's a bit difficult with the gong, you know, old girl,' he said ponderously.

'How do you mean?' Patricia leant forward a little, scenting a story.

'Well, it was all very hush-hush, you see,' he said.

'But I'm in the Service too, Reggie,' she protested. 'And you can rely on me. I'll keep my lips closed, promise.'

'Like your legs, I suppose,' Reggie said somewhat crudely, and guffawed.

'That's unfair, Reggie. Ever since we became engaged–'

'Yesterday!'

'Yes, yesterday. I've let you do it to me. I don't believe anyone should buy a pig in a poke – and I don't want you to make any of your crude puns about the expression please!'

'I wasn't going to, my dear,' the Colonel answered soothingly, remembering that half of Gloucestershire which could well belong to him one day, if he played his cards right. 'I was thinking about the gong, and whether I really dare tell you. And I've decided I can.'

'*Reggie!*' she breathed enthusiastically.

'Well, it was like this.' Colonel Hake-Smythe lowered his voice. 'You remember when our chaps went to Dieppe in the autumn, the commandos and those Colonial chappies?'

'The Canadians,' she prompted him eagerly, her eyes full of naked hero-worship.

'Yes. Well, who do you think was waiting for them on the beach when they landed?'

'Not you, Reggie?'

'The same,' the Colonel admitted, lowering his gaze modestly and thinking once more as his eyes fell on her black-clad knees, she's got a nice pair of pins on her!

'But what were you doing there, Reggie. I mean, how had you got there in the first place?'

'That is why his Majesty awarded me the gong, Patricia. You see it was like this—'

But Colonel Hake-Smythe was never fated to finish telling her how he had won his VC in France; for at that precise moment, the ancient waiter interrupted him, bending down stiffly so that the Colonel heard his bones creak. 'Colonel, there are two – er – gentlemen waiting to speak to you in the foyer … they say it's very urgent.'

'Fu—' Colonel Hake-Smythe caught himself just in time. 'Dash it all, can't a chap ever have a moment off!' He patted Patricia's hand, his dark sharp eyes already searching the restaurant for a way out and finding none. 'Just a jiffy and I'll be back. Help yourself to more bubbly.'

'I will, but hurry back, darling. I can't wait to hear how you won your gong.'

The military policemen were standing with their backs to the door: two big, slow-moving, serious men with hard, wary eyes that said they had heard it all before – and then some. 'Yes,' Colonel Hake-Smythe snapped in his best officer and a gentleman manner, 'what do you chaps want?'

'*You!*' the bigger of the two redcaps said.

Hake-Smythe faked indignation, his eyes searching desperately for a way out. But the two policemen barred the only exit – the door.

'I say, Lance-Corporal. You just can't talk to me like that. I mean you wouldn't be in the Military Police if you were blind. So can't you see *that?*' He touched his epaulette with an angry gesture.

'Yer,' the other MP said, a look of admiration crossing his hard face. 'And it's a load of Scotch mist. Come off it, Spiv, we've been looking for you for days. There's a general call out for you, mate.'

'But I'm Colonel.'

'Yer, *Colonel Bollocks!*' the taller MP interrupted him crudely. 'Now come on, get your skates on.'

Colonel Hake-Smythe gave in. The safe little refuge in the country and the prospect of half of Gloucestershire vanished as suddenly as it had appeared. When he spoke again, his voice was its usual, cheerful cockney. Holding out his hands, he said, 'Okay, it's a fair cop. Where to – the glasshouse?'

The bigger one shook his head. 'If I had my way, you'd be on yer way there before yer plates of meat could touch the deck! Sodding hell, nicking government funds, on the trot for three weeks, impersonating an officer and wearing a ribbon you ain't entitled to.' He shook his head, overcome obviously by the monstrosity of the grinning little cockney's crimes. 'For my money, they should put yer inside for the rest of yer natural.'

'But they ain't going to?' Spiv said quickly.

'No, you lucky bugger. Some officer named Cain wants to talk to you – *urgent.*'

Spiv, the fourth member of the Ultra team said a very rude word.

FOUR

Spiv touched his red-banded cap with his swagger-cane in his casual senior officer's salute. 'Sorry, I was held up. Good of you chaps to wait for me, though really you shouldn't have bothered.'

Captain Abel, seconded from the US Army's OSS, grinned at the little cockney's nerve. It had taken the Prime Minister himself to calm down the GOC London Area when the latter had discovered that no charges were to be pressed against the man who had stolen the Brigade of Guards' regimental fund three weeks before. 'You lucky stiff,' he commented, as Spiv lowered himself into the most comfortable chair in the little room.

'Ay, yer can say that agen,' Mac, the Ultra team's Scottish explosives expert growled, kneading plastic explosive with his thick fingers. 'In the old days, you'd have been for the high jump. By God, yer would!'

'Now, now, Mac,' Spiv said easily, 'don't go and blow a gasket. You know I've always been a jammy bugger.'

Cain who had remained silent up to now, banged his hook down hard on the desk in front of him, and barked, 'I know, and I'll have your guts for garters if you pull another bloody stunt like that, Spiv!'

'Sorry – *sir.*'

'Thank you for the "sir",' Cain said ironically. 'I'm grateful to you for having some little sense of military courtesy left. Perhaps it has escaped you that there are other officers present, eh?'

Spiv looked casually at a grinning Abel and Mac, whose ugly splinter-dotted face – the result of a mine exploding in his face during an op in France – was flushed a brick red, and said, 'I don't think they're worried about such things, sir. We're all pals in Ultra, sir. We don't go in for that kind of bullshit, do we, Mac?'

Mac's lips trembled violently. He seemed about to explode at any moment. Hurriedly Cain intervened. 'All right, you damned little rogue. Shut up and listen!'

'I'm all ears,' Spiv said and taking out the silver cigarette case which Lady Patricia had given him that morning after their first night in bed together, lit an expensive, hand-made Bond Street cigarette. 'Fire away, sir.'

'Thank you.'

'We've got an op,' Cain announced simply.

Mac's rage vanished at once. 'Now that's great, Cain,' he said enthusiastically. 'I thought we were going to sit on our fat rears here in London for the rest of the bluidy war! Where?'

'Switzerland.'

'Switzerland, mon!' Mac exclaimed. 'What's yon place got to do with the war, eh?'

'Yeah, skipper,' Abel, the ex-college professor, who was the team's language expert joined in. 'Since when has the shooting war spread to Switzerland?'

'It's not going to be that kind of an op this time, chaps,' Cain answered, and swiftly told them as much of Zero C's information as he felt it was safe for them to know. From the very first day he had been recruited into the Ultra team, Zero C had forbidden him ever to tell his men about the great de-coding operation. 'So, you see,' he concluded, 'we've got to prevent the Jerries from infiltrating the Soviet spy ring. And if they do, well we've got to take care of the – er – Jerry.' He shrugged carelessly.

Abel's eyes lit up. 'It's about time we did something for our Soviet allies,' he cried with that naïve all-American enthusiasm of his, which Cain disliked so intensely. 'They're out there, doing all the fighting in Russia, while we're nice and safe here, risking no more than getting run over by a taxi in the black-out.'

'There are one or two chaps doing a little bit of fighting in North Africa, you know, Abel,' he said coldly.

'But why is it up to us, sir, to prevent the Jerries from infiltrating the Russkies?' Spiv asked, his quick Cockney brain immediately seizing on the discrepancy in Cain's briefing. 'Why couldn't they have sent in a couple of their own strong arm boys? And why are we not supposed to have any contact with 'em, if we're supposed to be protecting them, eh?' He looked at the one-handed Major almost accusingly.

'Because it's too difficult for them to get their people right across Germany into Switzerland, Spiv, and because it's better for us not to be seen associating with their agents in Switzerland, in case the Jerries are already watching them, that's why,' Cain lied glibly.

Spiv, who before the war had run an underground railway out of Germany for German Jews – *with money* – and knew the Reich's borders like he did the East End's backstreets, looked knowingly at Cain. 'Come off it, sir,' he said contemptuously, 'ring the other one – it's got bells on it! Them borders to the east are wide open – open wider than a whore's legs!'

'Hush, mon,' Mac snapped, 'hush that dirty mouth of yours, will yer!' Mac, who had never looked at another woman since his wife had been killed by a German bomb in 1940, but concentrated all his violent energy on killing as many Germans as possible, squeezed a fist full of plastic explosive under Spiv's nose threateningly. 'Or I'll gie yer a taste of my knuckles. By God, I will.'

'All right, all right,' Spiv raised his hands in mock surrender. 'Don't get so aereated, Mac, or yer'll get your kilt all twisted.'

Mac muttered something in Gaelic, which sounded as if the crimson-faced Scot was preparing to carry out a second Glencoe Massacre. Cain stepped in quickly. 'Now that's enough of that – Mac ... Spiv. Let's concentrate on fighting Jerry and not each other. Now let's get on with it.' Swiftly he pushed on, leaving Spiv's awkward questions unanswered.

'Now this is the situation.' He tapped the small map of Switzerland he had pinned up on the wall behind. 'The people the Jerries will be out for, once they've got a lead on the Russian spy ring will be first, the boss Rado, located here at Geneva. Here at Lucerne, about a hundred odd miles away, there's the chap Lucy I've told you about. The Jerries might already know about him since he's a refugee from Germany – they keep check-lists of such people – and was peddling info to all and sundry in 1940. Then here at Lausanne, there's the third member of the ring, a Swiss journalist called Punter. He has useful contacts to the Swiss military and pumps them for information about the Jerries – they get it from their military attaché in Berlin. And finally we've got their radio operator, who floats around all over the place so that the Swiss radio listening service can't get too exact a fix on him. We don't know his real name,' he lied. 'But his code-name is "Jim".'

'Sounds English or American,' Abel said.

Deliberately Cain ignored the comment. 'They wouldn't exactly call him Vladimir,' he snapped. 'Would they now?' Abel flushed.

'Now this is how we do it. We'll go in with diplomatic passports. That should make it unnecessary to worry about things like residence permits; proof of ability to keep oneself. The Swiss are very keen on money, they tell me. Once we are through immigration, we ditch the diplomatic passes and use normal British passports and adopt the role of rich Englishmen – in your case, Abel, American – who are dodging the column and sitting out the war in safe, neutral Switzerland.'

Spiv beamed. 'Do you know, sir, I think I'm going to like this one. What are the Swiss judies like?'

'Sour-faced and riddled with clap,' Cain answered. 'Remember this is a military mission and not a Swiss bedroom romp, Spiv.'

'I'd rather fu–' Spiv threw a quick glance at Mac's glowering face – 'rather fornicate than fight, sir,' he corrected himself hastily.

'I bet you would,' Cain rapped. 'Now using that cover – and I'll see you are all plentifully supplied with money – each of you will take over one of the Russian agents. You, Mac, will be responsible for the journalist Punter. You, Abel, will watch Lucy himself. Spiv, you get Rado. I'll take the radio operator, the mysterious Jim. Later I'll give each of you an envelope, containing a photograph of the man you're dealing with and a list of all his known contacts. Switzerland's virtually an island these days since the war, so I could imagine that there won't be too many new faces popping up in our men's areas. I shall be in telephone contact with each of you every day and you will report to me immediately you spot a new contact, clear?'

'Ach, it's bluidy funny way to fight a war,' Mac grumbled, disappointed that he wasn't going to be killing Germans, but he nodded agreement like the rest.

Cain passed out the envelopes and added, 'each of you will put up in the best hotel in the place to which you are assigned. As long as you appear rich, no one is going to ask awkward questions in Switzerland.'

Spiv then asked his significant question. 'What are we to do, sir, if we find this Jerry infiltrator?'

Cain made the gesture of pressing a trigger with the forefinger of his good hand.

Spiv looked at him aghast, the envelope trembling slightly in his hands. 'You must be kidding, sir,' he gasped.

'I'm not,' Cain said firmly.

'But sir, you've just said yourself that Switzerland is a sort of island.'

'Yes.'

'Well, you know what that island's sur-rounded by? Not sodding water, but sod-ding Jerries, hundreds of thousands of them on all sides.'

'So?'

'So, if we knock this bloke and have to scarper for it,' he swallowed hard, *'where we gonna scatter to, eh?'* He looked up at the Major in white-faced, tense expectation.

But Cain remained silent. He had no answer for that overwhelming question...

DORA, LUCY, JIM AND OTHERS

'Five hundred years of democracy and what have they produced – a cuckoo clock!'

Graham Greene.

ONE

The city curled and bunched at the foot of the snow-covered mountains and spread itself along the winding shore of the river like a white snake basking in the dying rays of the winter sunshine. Soon it would be blackout time in war torn Europe; but in neutral Switzerland the lights still burnt brightly, exerting an irresistible fascination on Cain and Mac, who had not seen so many lights since 1939.

'Zurich, Spiv,' Cain announced, as the Spanish Air Lines three-engined Junkers 52 hit the tarmac. He dug the sleeping cockney in the ribs.

Spiv, who had fallen asleep, after a disappointing attempt to corner the flashing-eyed Spanish hostess in the rear toilet, woke immediately. 'Where's the judies, sir?' he asked, as the plane's speed started to slacken. 'I thought they'd be lining up down there waiting for new blood and the present I've brought them.'

A portly Swiss businessman in a striped pants and black jacket turned and looked at the little cockney, as if he had just crawled out of the woodwork.

Spiv stuck up his middle finger cheekily. 'Go on, mate,' he urged, 'give yersen a cheap thrill. Sit on that for me.'

The Swiss flushed and turned away hastily.

Then the plane came to a halt and they were unfastening their belts and filing down the gangway, out into the cold air, following the blue and white signs which led to the *Passkontrolle*.

Since the German victory in 1940, the Swiss, afraid that any apparent favouritism towards the Western Allies might draw Germany's wrath down upon her, had examined any plane which flew in from a neutral country with a fine tooth comb. Contrary to diplomatic custom, even those holding diplomatic passports, if their bearers were from the Allied countries, had to pass through immigration.

Now the Ultra team, lining up behind the mixed bag of returning Swiss, Spanish businessmen, and a couple of German officials from their Madrid Embassy, shivered a little in the cold echoing hall, watched alertly by a group of brown uniformed Federal Police in their high stiff caps, and machine pistols slung over their shoulders.

'Get a load of them rozzers, sir,' Spiv whispered to Cain. 'Hold me hand, *quick*. Don't they look wough!'

'Shut up, Spiv,' Cain snapped. 'Let's play this nice and cool.'

Cain wanted no trouble at this stage of the op. Everything about them was in order. They were perfectly clean except for the little 7.62 pistol which each of them had strapped to his inner thigh by means of sticking plaster. If the Swiss decided to search them, their mission would be over before it had even started.

'*Grüss Sie,*' the immigration official greeted them in his thick, guttural Swiss-German and then when he saw Cain's British passport added, 'Welcome to Switzerland.'

'Thank you.'

Carefully the official examined the passport, holding each separate page up to the light and studying it at some length. Behind him a Federal Policeman watched the travellers intently, his hand curled around the trigger of his sub-machine gun, as if he were prepared to use it at any moment. Cain took an instinctive dislike to him. The man's eyes were a brownish-green, slightly bulging and absolutely cold without a glint of expression – like a blind man's eyes. They were those of a born killer.

'May I ask you what your job in the British Embassy will be, *mein Herr?*' the official asked in his slow, careful English, still holding on to Cain's passport.

Cain took his gaze off the policeman. 'Clerk – I'm a clerk. All of us are.' He slipped his hook over the top of the desk so that the Swiss could see why he was obviously unfit for active service.

The Swiss nodded. 'I see.' He handed Cain back his passport. *'Merci, vielmals.'*

Cain breathed a slight sigh of relief and passed on towards the customs' table. Idly, the policeman with the killer's eyes sauntered after Cain and the others.

There was little worth smuggling from Spain, the poorest country in Europe, into rich Switzerland, and the customs' examination was cursory. Cain passed through swiftly, followed by Abel. Mac was next. Cain offered a silent prayer to heaven that the team's explosive expert had not decided at the last moment to conceal a lump of plastic explosive in his bag and pass it off as plasticine. But Mac passed through without hindrance. Now it was Spiv's turn. The portly customs man was about to wave him on too, without even a search, when his eye fell on to the magazine clutched under Spiv's right arm. 'What is this?' he demanded, pulling it from under the little cockney's elbow.

His mouth fell open and he gasped sharply as if he'd been punched in his fat Swiss belly when he saw the first picture in the magazine. Spiv had picked it up in Lisbon's red-light district during the team's one day stop-over there. 'Pfui,' he snorted from the depths of his Calvinistic soul. *'Pfui Teufel – was fur eine Schweinerei!'*

'It's better than the old five fingered widow, you know, mate,' Spiv said familiarly and winked knowingly at the disgusted official.

The man dropped the pornographic magazine as if it were red-hot. 'Go ... go,' he ordered, his double chins wobbling angrily, *'go now!'*

Spiv grinned and picked up the magazine. Behind him the Federal Policeman's cold eyes gleamed suddenly. The outline of a pistol was clearly visible against the thin material of the little Englishman's trousers. For a moment he told himself he should stop the Englishman; then he changed his mind. As casually as he could, he strolled over to the Corporal in charge. *'Brigadier,'* he said, 'all right if I go for a piss now?'

The Corporal nodded. *'Ja, ja.* But don't smoke more than one, understood?' He grinned.

Jean Muessli grinned back, but his killer eyes remained cold.

The number he had dialled in the *Rue de Montblanc,* Geneva answered at once. In High German, sharp, precise and very Prussian.

Swiftly Muessli explained what he had seen. 'Said they were clerks but they were soldiers of some kind all right; short hair-cuts, erect bearing and the like. And what

71

would a clerk be doing with a pistol taped to the inside of his leg, sir?'

At the other end there was a long silence. Muessli told himself that every minute cost money and he had always thought the Germans could make decisions swiftly.

Finally the other man broke his silence. 'Yes, I agree with you! Very strange, Muessli. Thank you for the information. There will be a one hundred franc note in the post for you tomorrow morning.'

Muessli's face lit up. 'Thank you, sir.'

'I shall be calling you again this evening at your home with further instructions when I've thought this thing out, Muessli.'

'In order, sir.' Hastily Muessli hung up before he would have to insert another precious franc into the box.

At the other end, a thoughtful *Oberkommissar* Heinz Pannwitz put down the receiver slowly.

TWO

It was a fine cold night. Over the broad expanse of Lake Constance the moon hung like a silver ball. It was an ideal place and time for their rendezvous. At this time of the evening and in this temperature, no one in his right mind would be walking along the banks of the great lake which separated Switzerland from Germany.

Foote, alias 'Jim', Cain's companion on the lonely walk, was a lanky man in his early thirties with mocking eyes, who looked as if he had made up his mind about the world; it was pretty much of a fake, but he wasn't too worried about it. As their shoes crunched over the frozen snow, the only sound save for the soft, sad lap-lap of the water to their right, Cain reflected how like most other agents he had met, Foote looked; the same surface wariness which was immediately noticeable yet with a streak of recklessness, even brutality, which was somehow also conveyed.

'The Old Firm took me in '37,' Foote broke the heavy silence, without looking at his companion, as if he felt it necessary to explain. 'They knew my views about the Reds. But I was clean, so it was no problem to get me into the Clement Attlee Battalion of the International Brigade.' He sneered suddenly. *'Clement Attlee,* what a name for a fighting formation!'

Cain said nothing. Jim's pale face and nicotine-stained fingers told him the strain the lone double-agent must be under. Let him get it off his chest, he told himself and kept on walking. 'When I came back from Spain, it was a walk-over to get myself recruited by the Reds in London. In '38 they sent me and a pal to Germany. There was some talk of us assassinating Hitler. I actually sat next to him once in a restaurant!' He laughed softly at the memory. 'Then when Hitler and Stalin signed their pact in '39 – what a nice bit of double-dealing that was! – they sent me to Switzerland and trained me to be a radio operator. Pretty cushy in those days,' he mused. 'Nothing going on, of course. Hell, nothing ever happens in this damned little country ... people only come here to die!'

'Tough?' Cain asked softly, breaking his silence for the first time since they'd left the tram which had taken them down to the deserted bank of the Lake.

'Yes. I've always got to be one jump ahead of the Swiss Army detector teams. Then there's the business of keeping Rado convinced that I'm a real Red. Last year he turned up at my flat, bearing champagne and when I asked him what the reason for the bubbly was, he nearly had a blue fit. It was the anniversary of the "glorious October Revolution!" And now, of course, I've got the Jerries on my back. It doesn't exactly make for steady nerves, Cain. But still,' he said with forced cheerfulness, 'nobody's taking pot-shots at me like they do at you.'

Cain smiled softly. 'Don't talk too soon, Foote. You never know.' Suddenly he decided he liked Foote; he could feel for him fighting this strange lone battle of his as a double-agent, regarded by the Swiss, the Russians and probably the English colony in Switzerland too, as a fool at best and a renegade at the worst. 'I can imagine it's not the easiest of assignments,' Cain said sympathetically, as they began to pass through a grove of snow-heavy firs.

'Oh, it has its compensations, Cain, you know. They made me a captain in the Red Army last month and awarded me the Order of the Red Bollocks or something or other.' He laughed a little bitterly. 'The hardest thing is the unreality of it. That's why I come up to the Lake every month or so.' He stopped and pointed to the faint glow on the German side of the Lake. 'That's Friedrichshafen over there. Big industrial city where they produce the subs that sink our convoys and the planes which knock hell out of our cities. I come and look at that to remind me that I'm really helping to fight the war and not playing games in this bloody little Swiss backwater.'

Cain could see just how vulnerable Foote was – how vulnerable all the members of the Ring were. They were living off their nerves; it would only be a matter of time before they cracked. At that moment it seemed opportune to ask the question he had been dying to pose ever since they had met one hour before. 'Who do you think it's going to be, Foote?'

'You mean the chap the Jerries are going to approach first?' Foote asked, shooting him a quick side-look.

Cain nodded.

'Punter's out. Good solid citizen with no weaknesses. Keeps his nose clean and counts his money in the bank like all these bloody Swiss. The Jerries have no reason to suspect him of anything.'

'I see! What about the boss Rado?'

'Well, he's clean as far as the Swiss authorities are concerned. He doesn't interest himself in politics and he pays his bills on time. He's got a nice map-making business going for him, drawing war maps for the Swiss newspapers, that sort of thing. Mind you the Jerries might be able to do something with his background, once they got on to him. I mean he's been working for Moscow for years now. And this country is lousy with informers who'd sell their own mother for a couple of Swiss francs.' He shook his head. 'But on the whole, in spite of his taste for high living, Rado's not the man most endangered.'

'That leaves you and Lucy,' Cain said quietly.

'*Me!*' Foote stopped and looked at Cain incredulously. 'You've got a lot of bloody cheek, Cain,' he snapped.

'You're vulnerable. And you can bet your bottom dollar that the Jerries got the list of all the members of the International Brigade. And you'll be on that list, Foote.'

'So what? I lie very low here in Switzerland. During the day I sleep and most nights I'm lugging that bloody radio transmitter all over Switzerland, trying to dodge the *BUPOs*.'

Cain wasn't altogether convinced, but he laughed sympathetically and said: 'Okay, I'll buy it.'

'You'd better.'

'So that leaves Lucy.'

Foote nodded hastily. 'Lucy is very dicey. The Gestapo must have registered him immediately on their want lists as soon as he did a bunk in '34. So he's a known quantity to them. Then he's not exactly kept his mouth shut since he's been here, and the Nazis have their informants everywhere. Sometimes I think half the folk in this rotten little country spend most of their time spying on the other half!'

Cain reflected that like all the other foreigners he had met in Switzerland in his brief forty-eight hours Foote hated the Swiss. All of them were plagued by the fear that one day when their money ran out, the Swiss would quietly boot them across the frontier to face the music back in the country from which they had originally come. The realization didn't make for a very happy relationship between the foreigners and the Swiss 'hosts'.

'And there's the business of money. Lucy's always attempting to peddle the bits of rubbish he picks up to the other embassies as well as to us – that is Moscow. And you can bet that the Jerries at their embassy watch everybody who goes in and out of the British or American embassies. Yes,' he concluded, 'for my money, Lucy will already be on their list–' He stopped short and pressed Cain's arm hard. *'What was that?'*'he hissed.

'What was what?'

'A noise. There was a noise in the firs over there.'

'Oh, come off it, Foote,' Cain snapped a little impatiently, knowing that the double agent was jittery. He shrugged. 'Probably some kind of animal?'

'Balls!' Foote snorted indignantly. 'An animal with two bloody big feet, you mean. Listen, there it is again!'

Cain cocked his head swiftly to the wind, his face abruptly hard and tense, his heart beating faster. Then he heard it – the soft shuffle of someone moving carefully through the snowy undergrowth, placing his feet down, heel first then the sole, so as to make the least possible noise. His hand flashed to his pocket and thrusting his fingers through the hole there, he pulled out the pistol strapped to his inner leg.

Foote stiffened. 'You mean–' he began, his eyes full of alarm at the pistol.

Cain held his hook up to his lips for silence, and whispered close to Foote's ear. 'Go in from the left. I'll post myself over there, near the fir with the broken branch.'

'You think–'

'Yes, I do,' Cain interrupted him firmly. 'Why else would anyone be out on a night like this in the middle of nowhere? Somebody's watching us. Now when I'm in position, I'll whistle once and then you move in. Make a lot of noise. That'll drive him in my direction. I'll be waiting for him with the gun.'

'And then?' Foote asked anxiously.

'We'll worry about that when we've got him. The Lake's big enough.'

'Oh Christ Almighty,' Foote hissed. 'I spoke too soon about this being a cushy number!'

'Off with you!'

Muessli didn't miss the whistle. He had been brought up on a poverty-stricken Alpine farm, from which he had escaped to the Federal Police at the first possible opportunity, and he'd never heard a bird call like that in his youth. Instinctively he crouched and dug his hands in his pockets hastily. His service pistol was at home and it could well be that the Englishman with the hook was armed like the one at Zurich Airport; and even if he weren't, that hook of his looked very dangerous. Swiftly, he packed the silver coins into his handkerchief and gripped them in his right hand. With the other, he took out the open packet of pepper.

In his youth on the farm, the only entertainment had been the brawls with which the Saturday evening country dances had usually ended and when the police finally turned up at the demolished *Gasthaus,* it had been unwise to be found with a knife or club in one's possession. Hence the pepper and innocent-looking coins, which were better than any imported American knuckle-duster. He tensed. The other man was running noisily through the firs towards his hiding place. Muessli knew the reason for the noise: the man wanted to drive him towards the waiting Englishman. In spite of his situation, Muessli smiled. The stranger was going to be in for a surprise.

Suddenly the branches to his immediate front smashed apart and the tall stranger appeared, chest heaving. He didn't hesitate. He lunged for Muessli. The Swiss reacted just as he had done as a farmboy when a youth had come for him in the crowded *Tanzsaal,* swinging a beer bottle. He ducked to the right. The pepper flew through the air. Foote shrieked as it struck him in the face. His hands shot up to his blinded eyes. Muessli didn't hesitate. His clenched fist, heavy with silver coins, went crashing home. It got Foote like the kick of a Swiss Army mule. His head seemed to zoom out over the Lake, and exploded in a sheet of violent flame. Muessli was running for his life before Foote hit the snowy ground.

'Okay?'

Foote looked up at his face and whispered thickly, 'Keep still – there are too many of you moving around up there.'

'Does it hurt much?' Cain asked, cradling Foote's head and lifting him slightly so that he could see the jaw better in the silver light of the moon.

'Only when I laugh.'

Cain smiled. Foote was a good sort. 'It doesn't look too bad,' he said, 'though you'll have a right old shiner there tomorrow morning.'

'Don't speak harshly to me, Cain,' Foote said, 'or I might just break down and cry. Here, give me a hand up, will you.' Cain helped him to his feet and handed him his handkerchief.

'Here, I've filled it with snow. It might help a bit.'

'Ta.' Gratefully Foote pressed the ice-cold handkerchief to his aching jaw. 'Well?' he asked. 'What do you think?'

'Can't you guess?' Cain said grimly.

'The buggers have rumbled us?'

'Yes.' Cain stared out across the gleaming lake towards the dark mass of Germany, *'those* buggers have rumbled us all right!'

THREE

Spiv spotted her immediately, as soon as she pushed aside the thick felt curtain, which attempted – and failed – to keep the cold out of Rado's favourite afternoon haunt the *Café du Lac.* She was tall, blonde and elegant, with a figure that had his eyes sparkling with interest immediately; she stood out a mile among the dowdy Swiss *hausfraus* and scruffy teenage students from the *Lycée* who frequented the lake-front café in the afternoons after school, and were Rado's reason for being there, or so he guessed.

Pretending to be busy with the thick cream cake, piled high with whipped cream, and the first he had seen in four years, he followed her progress. Hips swaying enticingly she crossed the room and took a seat at the big picture window just opposite Rado.

The little Hungarian spymaster looked up from the *Weltwoche,* let his greedy little eyes rest upon the blonde's excellent legs, then disappeared behind his newspaper again, shaking his head as if he knew that she was too good for him: he would have to remain content with the housewives and the spotty, giggling teenagers.

Spiv wasn't so sure. He took a sip of the ersatz coffee, the only thing in short supply, save fuel, in prosperous Switzerland, and waited.

He had been trailing Rado for three days now and found the job very easy. The little plump Hungarian was a man of exact routine. At 8.00 a.m. he went to his office, to supervise the cartographers and deal with his business affairs. At one o'clock he went to eat, always picking one of the heavy Swiss meat meals, complete with noodles and dumplings, which would have knocked Spiv through the seat of his chair if he had eaten one. At 2.00 p.m. precisely he returned to his office, leaving for the *Café du Lac* two hours later, to read the papers hanging from the wooden racks on the walls, and ogle the girls. Once a week he went out at night to visit his current mistress. Rado, Spiv had decided, was a man who lived by the clock, accounting religiously for every minute of his day. Even those he spent outside the marital bed, with his mistress.

Now he watched the blonde, as she picked at her cream cake delicately, unlike the fat, red-faced dowdy Swiss women all around who were digging into theirs as if it was their last meal on earth, and wondered whether he was right about her.

Up to now, he had not even considered the possibility that the Jerry contact might be a woman. Over the last three days his eyes had been fixed on the fat-bellied business-men who had approached Rado's table at midday and bowing and scraping with a lot of heavy Swiss formality had asked whether they could sit there. They had seemed to him likely candidates.

Now he realized he might have been barking up the wrong tree all the time. Rado, whose eyes always flashed from the paper he was reading whenever a woman entered the café, was wide-open to an approach from the female sex. *Was this blonde the one?*

Time passed slowly. Nothing ever hap-pened quickly in Switzerland, save for the rapidity with which money disappeared into the banks. Spiv already knew that. All the same, he could hardly restrain his impati-ence. If this woman were really the contact, when was she bloody well going to do her contacting? At five o'clock precisely, Rado would fold the last of the papers, which he read in four languages, reach for his grey Homburg and head for the door.

Spiv ordered another cup of the ersatz coffee in his atrocious French and flung a glance at the clock above the faded mural of a little boy urinating into a puddle with the legend below it. *'Never drink Water!'* It was almost ten to five and still the blonde hadn't made a move. Perhaps he had been mistaken after all?

And then it happened. The pale-faced blonde fumbled in her handbag for cigarettes. She took one out and placing it between her lips, suddenly discovered her lighter wouldn't work. She flicked it several times, her moist lips pursed in annoyance. But it refused stubbornly to light.

Spiv sat back and breathed a sigh of relief. The approach was as old as the hills. Before the war, he'd seen girls by the score use it at the local *palais de danse* or the *Mecca,* eyes already darting from side to side to check if their difficulty had been spotted by some likely male with his artificial silk scarf and *Brylcreem*-scented hair. More than once in those years, the lack of a match, a couple of foxtrots, a port and lemon and a 'fish an' tatie' supper had resulted in his landing in some nice warm judie's bed.

Rado fell for it. In spite of his bulk, he rose quickly to his feet, bowed and tendered the blonde a light, with heavy Central European charm, as if he were offering her a diamond ring.

The blonde smiled at him sweetly and said something Spiv couldn't quite make out, but he guessed she was speaking German. Rado remained standing, instinctively trying to suck in his stomach. He beamed down at her and said something which made her laugh. She tapped her useless lighter on the table, as if she were rapping out the morse code, the sweet smile still on her lips, her eyelashes moving up and down rapidly.

'Cor ferk a duck,' Spiv told himself, half in admiration, half in disgust. 'He's falling for it like a ruddy ton o'bricks! He'll be kissing her hand in half a ruddy mo!'

The next instant, Rado bent his greying head and pressed his lips to the blonde's hand, every inch the Hungarian gallant. She acknowledged the hand kiss with another of her fake, sweet smiles and rose to her feet too. She was half a head taller than the Hungarian. He nodded at the clock and reached for his hat, as she placed a five franc note on the table near the cup, without even a glance at the bill. Spiv told himself that she *couldn't* be Swiss; they usually examined the bill with the same intensity they studied the Bible on Sundays.

A moment later, the two of them went out together, chatting gaily, as if they were old friends. Spiv shot a glance at the wall clock. It was exactly one minute to five. The contact had been made with sixty seconds to go!

'*Na?*' Pannwitz snapped as she came in. It had been a worrisome day. First the call from Gestapo Mueller in Berlin; then the business of Muessli's run-in with the Englishman with the hook, whatever role he was playing. His nerves were a little on edge.

'Yes,' Rosamund Hirsch answered tonelessly. The animation of the *Café du Lac* had vanished now; her eyes were as dead as they had been the first time Pannwitz had seen her at Dachau. 'Yes, I picked him up.'

'Excellent, excellent,' Pannwitz rapped, and strode in his masterful way to the window. Somehow he was a little embarrassed. For years his only contact with Jews had consisted of a blow, a curse, a command. Now he no longer knew how to treat them out of the confines of a prison cell or concentration camp, especially when this one was a woman and a very pretty one to boot. In the end he turned and said simply, 'Well, woman, tell me about it. Don't just stand there!' She did so woodenly and without any emotion. When she was finished she stood there in silence, staring numbly into nothingness.

Pannwitz lit a cigar to cover his embarrassment and stared out of the window, absorbing her information. Rado hadn't been hard to find. After all the Gestapo had the records of the Hungarian Secret Police as well as those of the French *Sûrete* at their disposal these days. They had traced his career from his early days as an officer in the Bela Kun Red Army in Hungary, through Russia to Berlin in the late '20s. By that time, Pannwitz guessed, he had already been working for the Ivans. When Berlin had become too hot for him, he had transferred himself to Paris. In 1938 he had come to Switzerland. According to Muessli, he did fairly well from his map-making business, but not well enough to live the way he was living. Switzerland was a damned expensive country, as Pannwitz knew to his cost. There'd be all hell to pay in the *RHSA* accounts' department when he presented his expenses on his return to Berlin. So where was Rado getting the rest of the money he needed? It was obvious. From Moscow. There was no doubt in Pannwitz's mind that he was working for the Russians. But the question remained what was his exact role in their organization here in Switzerland?

Was he their pianist? [Gestapo slang for radio operator] That was always the best way to get one teeth's into a spy ring. Find the pianist and you could work from him, to find the rest of the organization. That was the way they had rolled up the Red Orchestra, once they'd arrested its pianist, Carlos, in the Rue Atrebates in Brussels.

He turned and looked at her. Her face was as wooden and remote as ever. Her spirit seemed completely broken. Unconsciously he nodded his approval, and pointed his cigar at her. 'Did he respond to the morse-code signal?'

She shook her head.

'Did you try more than once?'

'Yes,' she answered like an automaton. 'I tried a dozen times with my lighter, but there was no response. He must have just thought I was nervous.'

'I see. All right, you can go now. When's the next contact?'

'I'm to see him again tomorrow.'

'Good, we've got our foot in the door now. The fat Jew–' Surprisingly Pannwitz blushed. 'Rado, I mean, will lead us to the pianist yet.'

'Yes,' she answered absently, as if she had noticed nothing. Slowly she walked to the door. She turned, her hand on the knob, the door half open. From down below came the inevitable sound of some peasant yodelling on the Swiss National Radio. *'Ist was?'* he asked.

The light came flooding back into her pretty eyes again. 'You promise me nothing will happen to my mother?' she asked suddenly.

'Naturlich, naturlich,' Pannwitz lied glibly, his eyes fixed on the table, as if absorbed already in more important matters. 'I give you my word as a German officer.'

'Thank you,' she breathed and with that

she was gone.

'*Shit, shit, shit!*' Pannwitz cursed and rammed his cigar back into his mouth angrily. That very morning he had received an urgent call from Gestapo Mueller. Some damn fool of an official at *Theresienstadt* had put old woman Hirsch up the chimney yesterday. Now the Jewess, upon whom everything depended, was in a neutral country. And they had absolutely no hold over her whatsoever...

FOUR

Rosamund Hirsch looked at herself in the bathroom mirror. Like all lonely people, she looked at herself a lot in the mirror. The image reflected there took the place of other people's reaction to her.

The face that looked back had a wide, clear forehead, serious eyes, nervous flared nostrils and a pretty mouth which was not giving much away. It was a finely drawn face, taut and unhappy. For what seemed a long time she looked at herself, puffing nervously at her cigarette.

'My God,' she said to her reflection, finally, 'what are you doing? He is an ally and a Jew. Why are you helping those beasts

90

to trap him? *Why?*'

'Mother!' her image replied.

'Yes, mother,' she answered slowly, withdrawing her gaze. 'Always mother.'

She placed her cigarette on the edge of the bath and turned on the twin taps at full blast. She climbed in and felt the water flood up around her legs, jetting red-hot between her open legs, the steam rising and shrouding her fine breasts. She clenched her teeth, her blonde head thrown back in pain. But it didn't help. Rising from the bath, the tears streaming down her face now; tears of pain and self-disgust, she grabbed for the still burning cigarette.

In the steamed-up mirror she could see her tear-stained tragic face, as if through a grey mist. She took the cigarette out of her mouth. *'Du Schwein,'* she cried, *'du scheussliches Dreckschwein!'* Her face contorted with hate and self-disgust, she took the glowing cigarette and thrust its red-hot tip against the nipple of her right breast. Her scream was shrill and hysterical. Then the tension broke and she slipped to the wet floor, as she sobbed heart-brokenly at what she had become.

FIVE

Wednesdays they always held a *thé-dansant* at the *Café du Lac,* with music supplied by an Italian quartet, all flashing dark eyes, gleaming white teeth and pomaded, glistening hair. Rado never missed it. Now Spiv watched him as he danced to the sad little tune of that year *'Je t'Attendrai'* with the blonde – a head taller than he was – his plump body pressed close to hers, his knee jammed between her legs. Spiv told himself that the woman was definitely not Swiss.

The couples were dancing with each other on the small, circular floor, broad peasant faces red and sweating with exertion, as if they were back on the farm pushing a barrowful of potatoes up a hill.

The music stopped. The Swiss, grateful for the relief, applauded desultorily. The Italians were deeply moved. Immediately they launched into another tune. But the Swiss were already drifting back to their tables, each lit by a little red candle, although it was still quite light outside. A few couples, including Rado and his partner continued to dance, however, and Spiv decided it was time to get closer to them. If they were speaking German and not French as he thought they were, he might learn something. His alert dark eyes flashed around the room. There were a few middle-aged women, unaccompanied, watching the floor with hungry eyes. A couple of men of the same age group, who looked tired and grey. Probably from the effort of counting their money at night, Spiv sneered. Then he spotted the type he needed.

A fat girl in what was obviously her best black skirt and white artificial silk blouse, from which her enormous breasts seemed about to burst. He went over to her and bowed from the waist in the Swiss fashion. *'Dansez?'* He gave her that bold look which had brought him many a conquest in the local *Mecca* before the war.

The fat girl simpered. *'Oui.'*

With professional ease he thrust his right shoulder into hers and swung her onto the floor in his best tango style. She smelt of cheap scent, sweat and cows. 'Oh Christ,' Spiv cursed to himself, as she stepped on his foot for the second time, 'the things I do for sodding England! She must be straight off the farm.' But to the girl he smiled broadly, and said: *'Bon, hein?'*

She simpered again and whispered assent in a little girl's voice, although she must have weighed at least thirteen stone.

Now for the first time, Spiv could see the

93

tall blonde from close up, and could make out that she was answering Rado's patter in German. So he had been right. She was German after all. Even he could tell the difference between the thick, guttural Swiss German and the High German she was speaking. Yet, there was something about her that worried him, seemed out of place in a woman who was obviously spying for the Jerries. Where in hell's name had he seen faces like that before?

He swung in closer, circling Rado and the blonde, though not too obviously. The fat girl had rested her head on his shoulder, her eyes closed dreamily, her chest heaving with emotion or lack of breath. 'Oh balls,' Spiv told himself, 'now she's going to have an orgasm!'

Now he could begin to pick up oddments of Rado's conversation. 'I know a nice place ... just outside Geneva ... very discreet ... they don't ask for any identification... We'd be quite safe there, my dear...'

'The old bugger,' Spiv said to himself, 'he's already trying to get her between the sheets.' He flashed a look at the girl's face to catch her reaction.

It was prettily animated, a mixture of demure resistance and hesitant acceptance, as if she were having a struggle to overcome her suitably moral and natural female inhibitions. But her eyes were dead, Spiv thought, dead without any feeling whatsoever. Abruptly he realized she was playing more than the role her job demanded of her, the seductress. There was something else there. *But what?*

The woman was beginning to intrigue him – and annoy him, too. Who the hell was she and what was her real game? His smart, narrow face creased into a frown.

The fat girl stepped on his toes for a third time. She opened her eyes and looked up at him, her spotty face dizzy with instant love. *'Excusez-moi,'* she sighed and seeing the look on his face and thinking she was its cause, pressed him hard with her plump, muscular arm.

Spiv gasped for breath, feeling as if she had broken at least two ribs. He forced a smile. And then the music was ending and the couples were releasing their partners. The girl let go and took his hand quickly, as if determined not to lose him, now that she had found him. Obediently Spiv prepared to follow her. He couldn't do otherwise. She held his hand in a vicelike grip.

But Rado did not return to his table. Excusing himself to the blonde, he was hurrying towards a tall man waiting for him in the entrance to the *Café du Lac,* his plump face abruptly anxious, all thoughts of the intimate little rendezvous in the discreet hotel lost. The blonde stood there, seemingly undecided, tapping her right foot on the floor, as if angry.

The tapping seemed to startle the man waiting in the shadows. He swung round sharply, and Spiv caught a swift glimpse of a badly bruised chin, before the fat girl steered him purposefully to her table, as if she would never let go of him again.

Rosamund Hirsch put down the phone slowly. She had made her daily report to Pannwitz. But she hadn't told him what she had discovered in the *thé-dansant*. Of course, the man with the swollen jaw was the one Pannwitz was looking for. He was the pianist all right. He had responded instantly when she'd tapped out the signal. Rado had not even noticed the three dots and a dash of the letter 'V' which Pannwitz had told her was the sign of the Underground operator. But the tall man had reacted to it at once; she could tell that from the look on his face.

He was the one!

The blonde lit a cigarette. What was she going to do? Could she sacrifice them for the sake of her mother? Weren't they the very people who were trying to bring about the downfall of the National Socialist horror – while she was going to betray them to their enemies!

She looked at herself in the mirror, puffing nervously at her cigarette. Besides what guarantee did she have that Pannwitz would spare either her mother or herself once she had completed the mission?

In spite of the pink, soft-faced Gestapo officer's promise, she didn't trust him. In her last years with the Front Theatre she had met a lot of officers like Pannwitz – 'base stallions' the cynical frontline veterans called them. All clicking heels, hand kisses, *'bitteschoens'* and *'dankeschoens'*, who turned out to be nothing more than disgusting, greedy-mouthed, small-town lechers once they got a woman in a corner. No, Pannwitz would drop her immediately she had out-lived her usefulness, and leave her and her mother to their fates.

She stared at her image with cool, fatalistic eyes and told herself in a dry brittle voice. 'Let me tell you a couple of things. You're as good as dead anyway. So what have you to lose? There's got to be no panic, no hysteria now, *nix!* You've got to work this one rationally. *Ja?*'

The image did not respond. Suddenly determined, she stabbed out her cigarette and swinging round, seized her sling-bag. Opening it, she took from it the little map of Switzerland Pannwitz had given her back in Germany. She spread it out on the table in front of her, and stared at it intently, her pretty face very serious.

Of course, France was nearest. According

to the map it was only one hundred and fifty-eight kilometres to the first big French town, Lyon. But what did she know of the Swiss-French frontier? What kind of documents did the French border police and their German masters demand? She didn't know. Besides her French was elementary. How would she survive there, even if she did manage to get through?

She let her eyes roam across the map. Italy to the south. Turin? No, fascist Italy would be no better. Her gaze swung upwards. On the way into Switzerland, she and Pannwitz coming from Munich had crossed the frontier at Konstanz on Lake Constance. There had been a check, but her passport and Pannwitz's official papers had got them through without difficulty. She sucked her lip thoughtfully. But Konstanz was a small town and without any industry.

Her eyes followed the course of the German bank of the Lake. Not much in the way of inhabited places save small lakeside villages which had been popular with tourists before the war. Now they would be virtually deserted and inaccessible, as the ferry service between them and Switzerland had been stopped in 1939. Her eyes stopped at Friedrichshafen. According to the map it was the largest town on the Lake and she knew from Pannwitz that there was a once-weekly ferry service connecting it with

Switzerland 'to allow those damned Swiss profiteers', as Pannwitz had complained, 'to make money out of the Reich with their overpriced goods'. In other words, the service was run mainly for those representatives of Swiss firms which supplied the German war industry with the precision tools and spare parts it needed. Thoughtfully she folded the little map and replaced it in her sling-bag. Now she knew what she had to do. She would become an un-person once again, a shadow on the wall, a footfall in the night, a nothing.

She took up the pen and bent over a piece of the hotel writing paper. She dipped the pen in the inkwell and began to write, thinking out each word of the note with intense deliberation, for it had to be exactly right. *'Pannwitz, ich kann nicht mehr,'* she wrote. *'Das Spiel ist aus...'*

She paused then continued. It was the only way...

SIX

'By Christ,' Spiv was saying in mock fear, 'she had me up against the wall outside the ferking caff in a half-nelson afterwards! I can tell yer, gents, I thought me bloody number was up, that I did!'

Abel laughed heartily and asked, 'And how did you get away from your blonde Swiss bombshell?'

Spiv lowered his cheeky eyes demurely. 'I told her I couldn't. It was that time of the month.'

'Ach, mon,' Mac cried. 'Will ye no hold that filthy tongue of yourn!'

Cain only half heard the exchange. It was pretty obvious that the stranger with the swollen jaw that Spiv had seen in the *Café du Lac* had been Jim. He felt anger with him for having approached Rado in such a public place, forgetting the usual security precautions. Jim had obviously been more shaken by the attack at Lake Constance than he had realized at the time.

'I could see straight-a-flipping way,' Spiv was saying, 'that something had happened. Rado, this stranger bloke and the Jerry bint – all seemed to click off at that moment.' He looked puzzled. 'But sod it all, what went on between them, I haven't a clue.'

'What makes you so sure that the woman is German?' Cain asked, speaking for the first time since he had called them together to hear what Spiv had to report. 'And why do you think she's the infiltrator?'

'I *know* she is, sir.' Swiftly Spiv gave his reasons. The obvious way she had approached Rado, the ease with which she, a beautiful young woman, had let herself be picked up by the small, fat, middle-aged spymaster, her High German, her sudden acute interest in the stranger with the swollen jaw. 'She's in the game, sir. Not *that* game, but ours. I'll swear it.'

'Okay, I'll buy it, Spiv. Yes, I think you're right.' Cain pursed his lips thoughtfully. Hadn't Jim said that Rado liked the good life, in particular, women, though Jim had also said that the little Hungarian had some sort of sexual problem – he could only make love to Jewish women. But still, how could Jim know that? He pondered the problem, while the flat's wall clock ticked away the seconds of their lives with metallic inexorability.

Mac puffed at his pipe and blew a lungful of blue smoke at the low frilled lamp which hung directly over the table around which the four were grouped in heavy silence. He watched it flatten and float around the shade. 'What now, Cain?' he asked solemnly, 'what now?'

Cain looked at him, his hard face now sombre. 'It's obvious, isn't it, Mac?' He patted the automatic in his pocket with the side of his hook.

Abel went white. 'But not a woman, skipper,' he gasped, shocked, *'not a woman!'*

'Why not?' Cain answered, not looking at him. 'This is total war. Men, women and

101

children are killed on both sides.' He shrugged slightly. 'What's so different about a woman?'

'But there's somewhere we've got to draw the line, isn't there?' Abel rasped.

Cain did not answer.

Spiv sitting in the corner, flashed his quick dark eyes from the one-handed Major to the handsome young bright-haired American Captain. Cain and Abel! At that moment they lived up to their names: one, the hard-bitten realist, who was prepared to kill in cold-blood if he thought it was necessary without any moral qualms; the other, the moralist, the idealist, who believed in the inherent goodness of people, especially if they belonged to what Abel liked to call 'the masses'.

'But we're in this war to defend certain principles, aren't we, Cain?' Abel tried again. 'I mean if we aren't, then we're just as bad as them...'

His words trailed away, as Mac pointed his hooked pipe at him and said in a voice that was unusually soft and controlled, for him. 'Do you think the Germans drew a line when they killed my Rosie back in '40, eh, Abel? I'll ask you to answer that question. Did they question up there in yon airplanes that she was a woman?'

But Abel had no answer for that question. Instead he stared at the three hard English faces looking at him in the pool of yellow light cast by the lamp, feeling suddenly very American, cut off from these Europeans by his lack of experience; yet happy in a way that he lacked it; that he belonged to America, for all its naïve, idealistic, innocence. 'Okay,' he said lamely, letting his gaze fall to the table, unwilling to meet their eyes, 'you guys win. Let's kill her.'

Cain breathed out hard and Mac more heavily on his pipe. It was Spiv, who restored normality. 'Gent's,' he said very formally, 'may I point out one thing to you? The Swiss rozzers are going to be asking questions – a lot of the buggers – when they find out the bint has been done!'

Cain frowned. Spiv was right. Once they had put the girl out of action and Jim was then in a position to warn Rado that his pick-up was not all she had purported to be, they might well be able to leave Switzerland, knowing that their mission was accomplished: the Soviet spy ring would be proof against any further infiltration until London needed it no longer. But what if the Swiss police got on to them after the assassination, before the weekly plane left for Madrid on Monday?

Spiv seemed to be able to read his thoughts. 'It's now Wednesday, sir,' he continued. 'We'd have to pull it off almost at once and scarper next Monday. Otherwise they'd have another ruddy week to keep looking for us, and we ain't exactly been very good boy scouts these last few days. We must have left a trail a yard wide behind us.'

'All right, all right,' Cain snapped irritably, 'don't be such a bloody ray of sunshine!' He thought of the man who had spied on him and Jim at Lake Constance and knew Spiv was correct: they had all left a nasty big trail behind them, which wouldn't be too hard for the Swiss Police to follow. 'We've got to do it soon – and at the same time, we've got to cover our tracks.'

'I've got an idea, Cain,' Mac said, taking his pipe out of his mouth.

'You!' the other three said simultaneously.

'Ay.' Mac chuckled at the expression on their faces. 'Old Mac isn't always the bluidy bull in a china shop ye take him for, ye ken.' He rose to his feet, flashing a look at his wristwatch. 'But I must be off to the nearest chemist's before they close.'

And with that he was gone.

Mac worked steadily, pipe stuck in the corner of his mouth, while the others crowded into the flat's tiny kitchenette and watched in silence. First he had filled a cup with a mixture of four parts sugar and one part saltpetre – 'I told them in yon chemist, I needed it for curing bacon' – and now he was grinding the mixture with the handle of a kitchen knife. It was hard work and the sweat stood out in tiny opaque beads in his thick eyebrows. He had already finished making his first cup of mixture and was starting on his second.

Time passed steadily. Outside a grey mist had crept in from the Lake and curling itself around Geneva like a fat cat, had gone to sleep. The sound of occasional car tyres was muffled by the wet mist.

Now Mac was filling the powder he had prepared into two lead pipes, wrenched from the kitchen sink by Spiv on his instructions (after the water had been turned off). 'Primitive, but still effective enough,' he chuckled, not taking his eyes off the pipes. Finished with the filling, he groped in his pockets and pulled out two metal objects. 'Firing caps,' he explained.

'Where the devil did you get those from, Mac?' Cain demanded, as the purpose of Mac's activity began to dawn on him.

'In a wee country like this'un with no much room, save in the mountains, there's always plenty of blasting being done.' Mac shrugged and concentrated on fixing them in the pipes. 'So yesterday when yon Punter was having his afternoon kip, I had a walk in the hills to see what I could find. Ye never know when things like this could come in handy, ye ken.'

Cain shook his head. Ever since the ex-mining engineer had joined the SOE, he had spent all his free time devising ever more cunning and fiendish ways of killing Germans by booby traps and the like; explosives exercised an almost unnatural fascination for him.

Somewhat reluctantly, Mac unstrapped his wristwatch and put it on the table in front of him. 'It's a nice wee watch,' he said. 'Cost me all of thirty bob in 1934.'

'Oh, Christ,' Spiv said, 'don't break down and cry, Mac! *Thirty bob in 1934!* Brand new almost, ain't it? Shall we have a whip-round for you, Mac?'

'I'll gie ye a whip-around behind the lugs, if ye ain't careful,' Mac growled and began taking the watch's crystals out. Then he removed the hour-hand and stuck a steel plug to the face, setting it at thirty minutes after the hour.

Now all was silence in the little kitchen as Mac's skilled fingers made the last preparations, attaching the watch to a dry cell battery which he had removed from the flat's radio, and fitting the whole contraption to the tubes. He breathed out hard, and straightening up, flexed his shoulders.

'Well, there she is,' he announced proudly.

'What is it?' Spiv inquired.

'A bomb – a time bomb.'

'Eh?'

'Ay. When the metal of yon minute hand

106

hits the steel plug, the circuit there'll be closed. That'll make the electricity from the battery – there – fire the caps. And that'll be that. The bomb will go off.'

Cain admired the way the Scot had been able to build a time bomb out of odd materials within two short hours; yet all the same he was puzzled as to the purpose of Mac's creation. 'Do you mean us to use it on the woman, Mac?' he asked. 'I mean, I don't think it will be powerful enough for that, you know.'

'Of course, of course. I know that, mon,' Mac snapped. 'No, the little beauty,' he fondled the ugly device as if it were a baby's head, 'will be our cover.'

'How?'

'When we are finished with the woman, we plant this in her gas stove, hot-water boiler, central-heating oil tank – anything that is potentially – and *naturally*–' he emphasized the word, 'volatile! Thirty minutes after we leave, the thing goes off–'

'And the Swiss bogies,' Spiv interrupted, always quicker off the mark than the rest, 'will think that the woman was killed in the explosion.'

'Right, little man,' Mac answered.

'But doesn't that mean,' Abel said slowly, his face deathly pale, 'that we can't use a weapon? We'll have to kill her with our bare hands,' he looked down at his own hands as if visualizing them squeezing the life out of the German woman, 'so that they don't find a bullet wound on her.'

'Right,' Cain said.

'And when, sir?' Spiv asked.

'Tomorrow morning – *at dawn*,' Cain snapped.

Abel shuddered.

SEVEN

Cain crunched across the wet gravel, the sounded deadened by the fog. Geneva still slept. On the main highway there was a soft hiss from the trucks coming into town, bearing vegetables for the morning market; further away on the Lake, a foghorn was moaning like some monstrous animal wailing for its lost young. But the modernistic, white block of flats, in which the blonde lived, was fast asleep. There wasn't a light to be seen, save the low-wattage bulb burning over the entrance, fifty feet away.

Cain paused to pull on the pair of socks he had brought with him to deaden the sound of his boots. Behind him, Mac did the same. He was to come with him and force the door to the woman's flat open, while the other two kept watch at back and front.

They moved forward cautiously once more. Just before the door, he paused again, head cocked to the wind, trying to pick up any little noise – the swish of a broom, a soft monotonous whistle, the bubble of a pan boiling – anything which would indicate where the night porter would be. For Spiv had done his job of trailing the blonde well. Not only had he found out her address, he had also discovered what the set-up in the block of flats was. But he heard nothing. A moment later he discovered why. The night porter, an elderly man with a skin the colour of cold oatmeal, his yellow false teeth bulging slightly out of his wide-open mouth, was fast asleep behind the little desk, facing the two lifts.

Cain held his hook to his lips in warning to Mac. Together they crept by the elderly man, whose skinny chest rose and fell rhythmically. Instead of taking the lift to the fifth floor, they would get in on the first floor. That way they would not alarm the sleeping night porter. Carefully like two grey ghosts, they mounted the stone stairs. A few moments later they were in the lift and being whisked silently up to the fifth floor.

Mac tried the door gently. It was locked as they had anticipated, but the fact didn't worry him. He took the piece of pliable, but tough bakelite out of his pocket and slid it between the door and the wall. He grunted.

Once, twice, and applied pressure. An instant later there was a faint click and the door swung open gently.

Cain breathed out softly and looked at Mac.

Mac understood. He was to kill her, strangle her with his big, red hands. He looked down at them for an instant. Then he pushed his way through. Cain closed the door behind them.

Gingerly they felt their way through the grey gloom of the living room. An open door led off to the left. Through it, Cain could see the kitchen. He shook his head. Gently Mac eased open the door next to it. Again it wasn't the bedroom. They could see the outline of a toilet and bath. Cain pointed to the door on the right. That *must* be it.

Mac hesitated. Cain could hear him swallow distinctly and understood his feelings. He grasped the door knob and turned it. The door opened with a soft click. Over his shoulder Cain could see the dim rumpled outline of the bed. She was still sleeping soundly; she had heard nothing. Swiftly Cain pulled out his automatic in case anything went wrong, and watched as Mac crept ever closer to the bed, big hands outstretched, ready to grab for her throat, the instant she stirred, woke up, began to scream. His heart was racing crazily now. In

110

a moment it would start. She would attempt to spring up, eyes wide and staring with fear. The scream would die abruptly in her throat, as Mac's hard hands wrapped themselves around the soft neck. Her spine would arch, her mouth gaping wildly, but with no sound emerging save thick, stifled animal rasps as she was strangled violently to death. And then she would go limp, head lolled to one side, legs stretched out in one final agony, the life gone out of her.

Mac's hands sought for her neck in the mess of the rumpled thick feather-bed. He found nothing. *The blonde wasn't there!*

The next few seconds passed in hectic, frantic activity, as the two of them drew the curtains and switched on the light. All the rooms were empty. Angrily Cain flung open the wardrobe. Her clothes were in it. He ran to the dresser. Her sling-bag was in the top drawer. He fumbled it open. There was the usual female stuff – lipstick, eyebrow pencil, a handful of silver francs, a packet of German male contraceptives type *Vulkan* – and a return ticket issued by the *Deutsche Reichsbahn* for the stretch Munich-Geneva.

'Blast and damn it!' he cursed softly. 'Where in hell's name is she at this bloody time of the night?'

Mac shrugged. 'I dinna ken, Cain. Spiv swore she'd returned here after Rado had left. Saw her go inside and everything.'

'I know, I know,' Cain snapped impatiently. 'These one-horse Swiss towns pack up at eight o'clock. They go to bed with the chickens like the bloody farmers they are. There's nothing to keep anyone on–' He stopped short, as his eyes fell on the envelope propped up on the flower vase in the centre of the living-room table. 'What's this?'

He picked it up and read the words on the envelope. *'An den Herrn Oberkommissar Pannwitz!'*

'What's all that Jerry lingo mean in guid English?' Mac demanded.

Cain ignored his question. 'Get that kettle in the kitchen boiling, Mac,' he ordered.

'Eh?'

'Yes, I want it steamed open. I'm going downstairs to get the others. Now move it, man!'

Slowly Abel read out the contents of the little note in German, translating them as he went along. '*"Ich kann nicht mehr"* ... I can't go on. *"Das Spiel ist aus"* ... the party's over. *"Aber ich flehe Sie an"* ... but I beg you ... *"meine Mutter nicht zu toten,"* not to kill my mother... *"Es ist nicht ihre Schuld, dass ich ins Wasser geh,"* it's not her fault that I'm going into the water... Sarah Rosamund Hirsch.'

Abel looked at the others, his face puzzled.

'Now what do you make of that, fellers?' he asked.

Spiv was the first to react. 'She's Jewish! Now I know where I had seen that kind of face before – when I was running the underground railway in Germany before the war. About '38 they made all Jewesses stick a Sarah in front of their names.'

'Oh, come off it, Spiv,' Abel protested, his eyes full of disbelief. 'Gee, a Jewess wouldn't spy for *them*, the way the Krauts treat the Jews.'

'Perhaps they're blackmailing her,' Spiv answered. 'That bit about her mother, you know?'

Cain remembered what Jim had said about Rado's predilection for Jewish women and realized that it all fitted in: the Germans had obviously understood the value of using a Jewess as their infiltrator. 'She won't be the first Jew to have spied for the Nazis,' he said, 'and she probably won't be the last, whatever the Jews' reasons for working for them are. I mean, what better cover could they find for an agent – a member of a race they hate and persecute? Doors would be opened to that kind of person, everywhere in the Allied camp.'

'Okay, okay, I'll buy it, skipper,' Abel said hastily. 'But what are we to make of this note?'

Cain's face brightened slightly. 'Perhaps

she's saved us the bother of – er doing away with her.'

'What do you mean?' Abel asked.

'Put the note back where it was,' Cain ordered, 'so that the accomplice or her control can find it. After all it is her suicide note.'

'You mean that business of going into the water, sir?' Spiv asked, suddenly frowning thoughtfully. 'But why?'

'I don't know,' Cain answered and shrugged. 'Perhaps it all got too much for her. Rado's a Jew too, you know. Maybe she couldn't bring herself to betray him. God, I don't know – all I want to know is whether she has really done away with herself or not.'

'And how do we find that out, Cain?' Mac asked, looking down ruefully at his home-made bomb which wouldn't be needed now.

'The Lake. That's the only water around here. Come on, let's get down there before there are too many of those nosey Swiss around!'

They found her clothes half an hour later, piled neatly in the damp, white grass in front of a tumbledown wooden summer house. Cain picked them up curiously with his hook. There was a thin white dust coat of the type German women wore in the summer. A short, flowered dress, with puffed sleeves that Spiv said she had worn that afternoon at the *thé-dansant*. And a pair of brown leather gloves.

'But where are her bra and knickers?' Spiv asked suspiciously, the thoughtful frown still on his shrewd cockney face.

'People are still moral when they're about to die,' Mac growled. 'Remember what yer mother used to say to you when you were a bairn? Keep yerself clean underneath in case you're knocked down by a bus.'

Cain nodded. Many people were concerned about the appearance of their bodies after death. 'But why didn't she at least take her stockings off?' he mused aloud.

'Because she kept her shoes on till she reached the water's edge,' Abel answered his question for him.

They all turned. Abel was holding up a pair of high heeled shoes. 'Poor devil,' he said a little sadly. 'What a way to have to go. But I guess it was the only one out of the mess she was in.'

'Ay, poor lassie,' Mac said with an air of finality. He rubbed his wet hands together, as if washing them of the whole sordid business, 'that's that then.'

'Is it?' Spiv asked sharply.

They looked at him. 'What do you mean, Spiv?' Cain snapped.

'It's all as fake as a pair of tits on a Shaftesbury Avenue nancy-boy,' Spiv said contemptuously. 'First that business in the note saying she was going into the water. Hell, she was a classy bit of goods. That sort of stuff is the kind of bullshit Charlie Brown's missus writes when the old man doesn't come from the boozer on payday, to put the wind up him. *She* couldn't write anything like that. *Ner!* And why, if it was cold enough to put on gloves, did she wear that thin summer coat?'

'People are not usually in a rational state of mind when they're about to commit suicide,' Cain said.

'Natch,' Spiv answered eagerly. 'That's just what I mean. Why didn't she just slip into a pair of slacks? There was a pair hanging in her wardrobe, I saw 'em. No. Instead she went to all the trouble of putting on stockings and a frock and a coat – the whole works.'

'Come on, ye little rogue,' Mac growled. 'Spit it out, mon. What are ye saying?'

'I'm saying this. The whole thing is fake from start to finish. She left her handbag, but did we find her passport and any real money in it? Did we hell! So what did she do? She had another coat and another dress on underneath the dust coat, with her passport and money in the one pocket and a pair of shoes in the other. She did a bit of a strip here and then walked along the edge of the water for – say – a couple of hundred yards and then came out. I'll take even money that if we look to left or right of here, we'll find her footprints.'

'Well, come on,' Abel said, his face brightening at the realization that the Jewess might still be alive, 'let's go and find out!'

For a while it seemed as if Spiv were wrong after all. As the mist started to drift away across the Lake and the first dull white light of the new day began to fill the sky above the mountains, they searched the bank without success. Then Abel, out in front of the rest, spotted the larches growing close to the waters edge. 'Hey, fellers,' he called, 'come and look at this.' He tugged at a branch and held it so close to them that they could smell its typical sweet, sooty odour. 'See there. Somebody's held on to that. You can see where the bark had been rubbed off a bit.' He let go of the branch and it swung back to its original position, less than four foot above the water. 'Get it?'

'Of course, she pulled herself out with that,' Cain exclaimed.

'We used to pull the same trick when I was a kid,' Abel said. 'Vanishing into the third dimension we called it. Up into a tree and then into the next one – there – and perhaps on to another like here. And down to earth again. Here you are – the woman's footprints!'

They crowded round him in the thick clump of larches, while Spiv lit a match so

117

that they could see better. There were clear imprints of two soles landing heavily on the wet grass and a lighter trail leading up the bank.

'A very resourceful young woman,' Cain said softly.

'Ay, ye can say that again,' Mac agreed. 'But what in heaven's name is she about?'

'Well, for sure she's running away from that guy Pannwitz,' Abel said.

'Yer,' Spiv breathed, almost as if he were talking to himself. *'But where the sodding hell is she running to? A Jewess on the trot in Europe today...'*

EIGHT

She left the ferry which had taken her across Lake Constance without difficulty. Her elegant winter coat with the fur collar and her smart Berlin accent had their effect. The portly middle-aged official in the light green of the Frontier Police beckoned her to the front of the crowd of nondescript Swiss travellers with a courteous *'Bitte schoen, gnaedige Frau.'* He stamped her passport with only a perfunctory glance at it and after she had told him that her destination was Berlin, wished her a *'gute Reise.'* A moment later she was striding across the cobbled jetty, leaving behind her a crowd of silent Swiss, who had abruptly become aware that they'd left the security of their nice little neutral island to enter a frightening new world, fraught with danger.

Rosamund Hirsch walked towards Friedrichshafen's main station slowly, her face calm, but her mind racing, as she went over the details of her plan once again.

Military vehicles, filled with hard-faced men in steel helmets, sped by. The pavements were crowded with others in field-grey and the mauve-blue of the *Luftwaffe*, most of them attached to young women in short skirts and knee-high boots, who clutched their arms frantically, as if they already knew that this was the last time they would see their men alive.

But Rosamund Hirsch had no eyes for them nor the elegant, bemedalled young officers in their gleaming riding boots. who looked at her with admiration as she passed. Her gaze was on the grey landscape of ruined factories and dwelling houses on both sides, as she got closer to the station. It was a very good sign. It fitted in exactly with her plans.

She had fifty marks for her ticket and nearly a thousand Swiss francs. She would change them later on the black market, where she could get a higher rate than the official one; there were already plenty of people who had seen the writing on the wall and were hoarding foreign currency against the day when the One Thousand Year Reich would fall apart. With that money she would be able to keep herself in the little hotels with which the place abounded, until the first raid.

Then she would hurry to the nearest bombed street, and note the first name she saw on the door of one of the ruined apartment houses. With that information she would go to the usual emergency committee set up after such raids and state that she had lost her identity card and ration book. She knew from her days on the run before Dachau, that people in such committees were so overworked that they had no time to check. With her new identity card and ration book, she would take the next train to Berlin, the easiest place in wartime Germany to begin to go underground.

But first she had to throw Pannwitz off her track. For she had no illusion that he wouldn't tumble to her little trick soon and take up the chase. Once he realized, with the aid of his agents in the Swiss Police, that she had left Switzerland and headed for Germany, he would guess immediately that she would try to find a big city to hide in. He knew the ropes, as well as she did. Therefore she must encourage him to believe that she had headed for the nearest one – *Munich.*

She pushed her way into the 19th century station, filled with the usual flotsam of wartime: lordly officers, smoking cigarettes and talking in overloud voices; weary shabby infantrymen, laden down by weapons and kit, returning to the front and surrounded by their red-eyed womenfolk and crying children; pale-faced, bespectacled military clerks and officials, different coloured bands around their arms to proclaim their function; poorly dressed civilians, clutching their pathetic bundles and parcels, as if a thief might remove them at any moment; and everywhere the hard-eyed, helmeted Field Gendarmerie, the silver-plate of their office around their stiff necks – the 'chain dogs'.

She passed a couple of them, feeling their steely gaze fixed on her, but telling herself that it was only her imagination – they were looking for deserters from the Army – and joined the long line in front of the ticket office.

A quarter of an hour later, she had her third class ticket to Munich and was walking over to the slot machine which gave out platform tickets. She slipped in a ten pfennig coin and clutched the ticket hastily as it popped out. Swiftly she slipped it into her pocket and fought her way through the throng of soldiers and civilians to the ticket collector. He clipped her ticket without looking up and she passed through. Before her she saw the usual security check-point that was to be found on every large German station: an artificially constructed narrow passage of wooden boards, painted white and lit by arc lights. At either side there were the 'chain dogs' with their rifles slung over their shoulders, and next to them, two older men in long ankle-length leather coats with hats pulled down over their faces. Gestapo!

She swallowed hard and then told herself she hadn't been an actress for nothing. 'Keep smiling,' she commanded herself. '*Smile* – damn you!'

Her pretty face beaming as if she hadn't a care in the world on this grey wartime morning, she sailed past them, as if completely unaware that they even existed. Behind her she heard one of the Gestapo men whisper to his colleague, 'Look at the legs on that one. I bet they go right up to her pretty little waist.'

His colleague goggled and she was through.

The morning train for Munich started to steam slowly into the station, the locomotive bearing the usual patriotic legend of that year. *'Raeder Rollen fur den Sieg.'* Up in the roof, long bereft of its glass by the air-raids, the loudspeakers began to echo hollowly.

'*Zug nach Munchen ... weiterfahrt nach Berlin, Richtung, Breslau,Warschau...*'

'Good,' Rosamund told herself. The train would be taking on leave-men on their way back to the front. It would mean she would have better cover.

With a squeak of rusty brakes and a sudden cloud of steam, the locomotive rolled to a stop. Immediately the crowd surged forward, eager to get a seat. For some of them – the men returning to the Russian front – there were days of travelling ahead of them and they were determined to obtain a place by any means. Eager soldiers, ignoring the protests of red-capped guards and angry civilians, swung themselves aboard and raced down the corridor to reserve seats for themselves and their comrades, flinging bits and pieces of equipment everywhere in the compartments to do so. Windows were thrust open. Outside their waiting, shouting, struggling comrades, thrust in their packs and heavier equipment, while here and there other soldiers heaved themselves up into the net racks; the best place in the train to get a good undisturbed sleep. In an instant, all was the usual wartime station chaos – exactly as Rosamund Hirsch had hoped it would be.

Boldly using her elbows, not caring when the laughing, sweating soldiers used the confusion to feel her breasts or press their bodies against hers, she forced herself through the throng until she reached the usual compartment on every train with three black circles on a yellow background. This indicated that it was reserved for badly wounded men. As she had anticipated it was empty. She did not hesitate. Hastily she reversed the coat, which because of the wartime cloth shortage had been cunningly designed with a different colour on each side. Thus the German woman, limited to one coat for an indefinite period had, in reality, two coats in one; it was a very popular fashion in the year 1943. Now, instead of a black coat, she was wearing a deep red one. She took off her hat and pitched it under the seat. With one hand she held up her blonde hair and with the other she bound it up with the headscarf she had taken out of her pocket. Already the guard was shouting his usual formula on the platform. 'Everybody clear of the train... The train will leave in exactly...' She had only a minute left.

She took the powder compact out of her pocket and flung white powder onto her face wildly.

'Bitte Vorsicht bei der Abfahrt!' the guard was calling outside.

She took one last glance at herself in the mirror. She looked as she had hoped she would – a rather badly made up working class girl who had come to see her boyfriend off to the front. 'Now cry – *you bitch!*' she ordered herself and opening the door, the tears already beginning to well up in her eyes, she dropped to the platform again once more. She was greeted by the usual wartime parting scene. Shrouded in steam, the women were already waving their handkerchiefs or sobbing into them, while soldiers, some numb with sadness, others laughing wildly, were leaning out to them.

She paused in front of a group of happy, drunken young men with the black and white ribbon of the *Liebstandarte* around their sleeves. A handsome, blond young SS man, who didn't look a day over seventeen, bent down towards her, emboldened by his comrades, and cried: 'Give me kiss, blondy. I'm off to Russia!' He pursed his lips hopefully. She reached up on her tip-toes and felt his tongue slide between her teeth greedily, as if the boy were seeking some last human contact before it was too late. For a fleeting moment, their eyes met – those of the SS man and the Jewess – and they both recognized the fear that haunted the other; then the train began to pull away, carrying with it the boy who would not survive the spring campaign.

Suddenly she found she was weeping genuine tears. She waved hectically as the train gathered speed and melted to one long blur before her tear-filled eyes. A moment

125

later it was gone, just two red lights disappearing round the bend in the line.

Sadly the women began to trail back to the exit, grey sobbing ghosts in the loud, echoing, steam-filled silence. Rosamund Hirsch went with the rest, damp handkerchief pressed to her tear-stained face. The 'chain dogs' and the Gestapo men did not even look at her. A moment later she had dropped her platform ticket in the collector's box, and was passing outside.

Thirty minutes later, her tears gone, she was standing in front of one of the many little hotels which surrounded the station, places where one paid in advance and where no questions were asked when a soldier and his girlfriend asked for a room for an hour only. The *Hotel zum Adler* was no different, save for its grandiose name for such a shabby, run-down place and the notice it bore in its window. *'Juden unerwunscht.'*

She smiled slightly and straightening her shoulders, seized the door handle. Sarah Rosamund Hirsch had gone underground once again...

A TRIP ACROSS THE WATER

'Often most valuable clues can be picked up by spies who get beneath windows and peer in at the corners at critical times.'

William Le Queux.

ONE

'Stehenbleiben!'

The order came harsh, decisive, and immediately arresting. The four Ultra men swung round. Two brown-suited Swiss police stood there at the exit to Geneva's Main Station. The pink-faced one had a machine-pistol slung under his arm; but the other already had his pistol out. And the way he held it convinced the four Ultra men he meant business. Crouching slightly at the knees, he was holding it at arm's length in both hands, his brown-green killer's eyes daring them to make a move.

Slowly the four of them started to raise their hands, while the crowd of Swiss workmen, carrying their lunch in smart brown attaché cases, parted on both sides of them in alarm.

The one with the pistol jerked it in the direction of the wall. He didn't have to speak. They understood the gesture well enough. Obediently they placed their hands against the wall and spread their legs slightly.

Rapidly he ran his free hand down their bodies. He was an expert. He missed nothing. He found Cain's pistol at once, as if he knew exactly where to look for it. 'All right,' he snapped in German, 'take it out – *slowly and carefully.*'

The fact that he spoke German surprised Cain; he thought the Geneva Police would have been French-speaking. But the policemen did not give him much time to consider the matter. Jamming his muzzle painfully into Cain's kidney's, he rapped, 'Clear?'

'Clear,' Cain gasped.

One by one the smaller of the two policemen disarmed them and took their passports, passing his booty to the one with the pink face.

'All right,' the policeman snapped, 'put your hands down, but careful. We're taking you in.'

'Why?' Abel protested.

'*Why?*' the Swiss sneered. 'Not a residence permit among the four of you and illegally possessing weapons! Isn't that enough?'

'That's enough,' the pink-faced one said, speaking for the first time. 'Get in the back seat of the car – *slowly!*'

The smaller one opened the door of the big, black pre-war Peugeot of the kind used by the French and Swiss police, watched by a couple of gaping workmen and a boy in knickerbockers and stocking cap, whose shining eyes already reflected the exciting story he would be soon blurting out to his parents about the 'gangsters with real

130

pistols, *honest!*'

Spiv winked at him, as he entered the car, and said in English out of the corner of his mouth, 'They call me George Raft, kid.'

'Hold your trap!' the smaller of the two policemen snapped and took his seat next to the driver, his pistol still levelled at them.

Cain looked at him. There was something faintly familiar about the man's eyes, but he couldn't recollect where he had seen him before – if he had.

'And remember, the four of you,' the Swiss continued. 'No tricks or I'll blow your heads off.'

'Must you keep pointing that damned cannon at us?' Cain asked him, as the other Swiss slipped behind the wheel. Cain's mouth had suddenly gone very dry. He stared obsessively at the blue-black muzzle, as if by means of concentrated will-power, he could send it and its owners to all hell.

'Shut up,' was the Swiss's reply.

'You're a great conversationalist, anyway,' Spiv said with forced cheerfulness.

The pistol swung in his direction. 'Okay, okay,' Spiv said swiftly, 'I surrender.'

The pink-faced Swiss thrust home first gear and took the car away from the kerb. He drove fast. Through the centre, jumping a red light, which was hardly correct for a policeman, Cain couldn't help thinking, and then through several narrow side streets.

Almost before they were aware of it, they were out of the city centre and were heading fast for the snow-capped mountains.

'Hey,' Abel protested, 'what gives? This isn't the way to the *Palais de Justice*.'

'The things you say!' the pistol-carrying cop sneered, showing a mouthful of dingy, sawn-off teeth.

Now Cain remembered where he had seen the man with the killer's eyes. At Zurich Airport the day they had arrived in Switzerland! Suddenly his mind started to race.

Sitting next to him Abel seemed able to read his thoughts. 'The driver's not even Swiss. He's German, skipper,' he whispered.

'Balls!' Cain cursed. So that was it. The Swiss were in the pay of the Germans. Now the two of them were going to try to bluff their way across the frontier to Occupied France and deliver them to the Gestapo. France couldn't be more than thirty miles away now. Wildly he cast around for some means of escape, as the car roared higher and higher up into the mountains.

But he was wrong about the vehicle's destination. Half an hour after they had left the station, the driver got off the main road, forking to the right. They raced by some very modern wooden bungalows, obviously summer homes for rich Geneva people, and then began to slow down as the paved road gave way to a frozen rutted track. They were over a thousand feet high now and below them Geneva and the glistening lake were spread out like an aerial photo.

For a further five minutes they bumped and rattled over the track until they entered a thick fir forest, the trees' spiked tops still heavy with frozen snow. Abruptly the pink-faced one applied the brake and stopped. But he didn't turn off the engine. Looking at them in the rear-view mirror, he said, 'Why were you asking those questions at the station?'

'What questions?' Abel asked with feigned innocence.

The pink-faced one nodded almost imperceptibly. The other cop brought down the muzzle of the pistol on Abel's hand – hard. The American yelped with sudden pain.

Cain realized that they were in trouble – real trouble. 'We were trying to find out if the girl was a friend of ours,' he lied unconvincingly.

'Since when did Englishmen have German girlfriends?' Pink-face sneered.

Cain stayed silent.

'And even if they did, did you think you might pay her a little visit in Munich?' Pink-face laughed. It wasn't a very pleasant sound.

So the Gestapo – and he knew instinctively he was dealing with the Gestapo now – thought the blonde had gone to Munich, Cain realized, and they were looking for her, too. Her plan to disappear had been the real thing.

It had not been hard to follow the girl's escape route out of Switzerland. The Germans only allowed people wishing to enter Occupied Europe from Switzerland to cross the frontier at certain specified points: Geneva itself if they were going to France and Schaffhausen, Konstanz and Friedrichshafen if they were entering Germany. And in order that the Germans could get their hands on as much urgently needed Swiss currency as possible, travellers were only allowed to book their tickets to the frontier. From there they would have to buy new ones from the *Deutsche Reichsbahn* in order to continue their journey, in Swiss francs of course. Thus it hadn't been hard to trace the route of a handsome, elegant blonde German woman, who had booked her ticket to Friedrichshafen at a surprisingly early hour the day before.

Obviously the two cops knew that too. They knew too that the woman had gone on further to Munich and they were after her. Now seemingly they were tidying up the loose ends left in Switzerland. But did they know about Jim? Had the girl told them about her seeing Jim and Rado together at the *Café du Lac?* Pink-face's next question told Cain that they didn't, for he asked: 'Now who was this fellow you – the one with the hook – met at Lake Constance on Tuesday?'

The other three looked at Cain. He shrugged casually. 'Just a chance acquaintance.'

'At eight o'clock of a pitch-black winter's night? You'll have to think of a better lie than that, Englishman.'

'*Ja,*' the one with the killer eyes agreed. 'And you were worried enough about being overheard to try to kill me, weren't you, Englishman?' He sneered. 'Now the boot's on the other foot. We do the killing.'

'Not yet, Muessli,' Pink-face snapped.

'Sorry, sir.'

'What exactly is your game, you with the hook?' Pink-face asked, his eyes reflecting his angry bewilderment in the rear-view mirror. 'What's your connection with the Reds?'

'Reds?'

'Yes, you know what I mean! Why is an Englishman, probably a member of the well-known Secret Service, interesting himself in the activities of the Red Secret Service in neutral Switzerland?' Pink-face feigned a smile. But not very successfully. 'If you tell me, I might be persuaded to call off my blood-thirsty friend here.' He indicated his companion. 'Talk and you can walk back to Geneva. Keep silent and they'll be carrying you back – when they find you – in a wooden box.' He flashed a glance at his watch. 'And make it snappy. I'm heading for the Reich in a couple of hours to help find that treacherous little blonde bitch.'

Cain felt his heart begin to beat like a trip-hammer. Once he started to talk, he knew they would pump him and pump him till they had everything, even if they had to smuggle him out of Switzerland into the Gestapo's torture chambers to do so. Then they'd have the secret of Ultra and the whole course of the war against Germany would be changed. Britain would be blind again, just at the moment when she was preparing for the invasion which would bring about the end of Nazi domination in Western Europe. What the hell was he to do? Could he sacrifice the lives of his three companions for something they didn't even know about? For a second he wavered, but only for a second. Ever since he had joined the SOE, he had told himself that he must be prepared for this moment.

While the others stared at him, their faces suddenly very pale, he said slowly and deliberately, forcing himself to keep his voice calm, 'I know nothing. If you are going to kill us, do it now – and get the damned thing over with.'

Oberkommissar Pannwitz stared at the Englishman's ashen face in the mirror. The man was mortally afraid; he knew that. In these last years he had discovered that he could virtually smell fear. Yet all the same, the Englishman had that desperate bitter look in his eyes, which told him that he would not break easily. In the end he would of course – they all did – but for that he needed the equipment and the time. And he had neither. Bormann and Gestapo Mueller had been screaming for results ever since he had discovered that the Yiddish bitch had not committed suicide, but was attempting to go to ground in the Reich. Obviously she had discovered something very important. Why else would she run like that and risk her mother's life? He must get back to Munich and take charge of the massive *razzia,* which was being planned for the morrow. He made his decision; he had no further time to waste on the strange Englishman and his companions.

'Muessli,' he commanded.

The Swiss cop knew exactly what the swift look the German gave him meant. 'Yessir,' he snapped. 'At once, sir.' The risk he was now going to have to take meant money – big money for him. Suddenly he was very happy. 'Get out, one at a time, by this door.' He indicated the one behind him. 'And *slowly!*' He flashed them his dingy, sawn toothed smile. 'I shall be watching you all the time.' He opened his own door and got out, eyes hard and intent, pistol levelled at them.

Abel got out first, followed by Cain. Then Mac. Spiv was last. Just as he was bending under the doorjamb, his felt trilby came off, dislodged by the door. He paused there, hands frozen in mid-air, as if waiting for an order to pick it up.

'Move it,' Pink-face commanded. 'I want nothing left in the car.'

'*But slowly,*' Muessli said. 'No tricks.' Already his mind was working out the kind of interest rates he could demand from the *Credit Suisse* on a large sum. Perhaps if he decided to put the money in for a longer term they'd give him a higher rate of interest. Or might it not be better to buy *Obligations?*

But Jean Muessli never did work out that particular sum. For as Spiv bent to pick up his hat, he straightened up with surprising speed, and whipped the trilby's rim across the cop's face.

Muessli screamed shrilly and hysterically like a woman, and fell back, hands clutched to his face, the bright red blood jetting between his tightly clenched fingers.

'Move!' Cain yelled.

He sprang forward and brought his hook around Muessli's neck. He pressed hard. The scream of fresh pain was stifled abruptly as the hook bit deep, deep into the Swiss's flesh. In the same moment that Mac grabbed at the door to the driver's seat, Cain tore through Muessli's windpipe. He died without another sound.

Pannwitz thrust home first gear. Desperately Mac tried to get the door open. To no avail, Pannwitz put his foot down hard on the accelerator. The black car shot forward. *'Bugger it!'* Mac cried and dropped off to the ground, as a panic-stricken Pannwitz narrowly missed a tree in his desperate attempt to shake off his attacker. Then giving the engine full power, swerving from side to side crazily, as if he anticipated pistol shots, he disappeared out of sight.

With a soft, horrible sucking noise, Cain withdrew the gory hook out of the bloody mess which had once been Muessli's throat and allowed the dead Swiss to sink to the ground. Next to him Abel lowered the dead man's pistol. 'Thanks, Spiv,' Cain said, hardly able to contain his voice. 'You saved our bacon that time.'

'Razor blade … razor blade in the brim of the hat,' Spiv's voice was not too steady either. 'Trick I picked up in the East End before the war… Rozzers could never book you for an offensive weapon, see.'

Cain nodded slowly and looked down at Muessli.

Abel looked at him and then at the corpse.

'I guess we'd better bury him, eh, skipper?'

Again Cain nodded, 'Yes.'

But no one moved. They were still too shocked, it seemed, by the events of the last few minutes and their implications. In the end, it was Spiv who made the first move. He dropped Muessli's stiff brown cap over the mutilated face with the broken false teeth lying next to it, like two halves of a grin. 'I've had enough of looking at you, beautiful,' he said and then walking a few paces, picked up a broken branch, and started to scratch away at the frozen earth. 'It might not be a bad idea,' he said after a few moments when they had still not moved, 'if you gents sort of gave me a hand. After all we've just gone and killed a Swiss rozzer, and I don't think his pals would like it too much, if they found out.'

Numbly, the three others found sticks too, and began to help him.

TWO

They were about half a kilometre from the lakeside village when Jim thought it safe enough to hand him the parcel containing three pistols for the others. 'Belgie,' he explained. 'Won't stop anything much over

140

twenty-five yards. The Swiss are pretty hot on illegal weapons.'

'Thanks, Foote,' Cain said gratefully and accepted the parcel without stopping. 'I appreciate it.' He tucked it almost casually under his arm and strolled leisurely on at Jim's side, as if they were two ordinary visitors to Lake Constance enjoying the first welcome rays of the spring sun; yet one was a double agent and the other, Cain, was a wanted man since that morning.

'What do you want them for?' Jim asked after a while.

'We need muscle. That Jerry got away with ours and I don't trust anybody in this damned country. They can all be bought.'

'You can say that again,' Foote agreed and cast a nervous look over his shoulder down the path, as if he half expected to see a Gestapo assassin trailing them.

'Don't worry, Foote, they're not on to you, *yet.*'

'But they bloody well soon will be, once they get their big Jerry paws on to that girl. I could kick Rado up his fat Jewish arse for ever getting involved with her. Just now, too, when Kursk is really hotting up. Yesterday I received more than a dozen intercepts from Dansey, which the Bletchley boffins had sent him.'

'The big spring push?' Cain asked. Somewhere he could hear the hollow thump-

thump of a big drum and the muted blare of a brass band.

'Definite. The Jerries are sending all they've got to the Central Front. Bletchley says it's the biggest panzer army ever assembled. A couple more weeks and the boffins will have put the whole bag of bones together for the Russians. After all, they don't call them the Shadow German High Command for nothing.'

'Yes, I suppose so.' The sound of the music was getting louder from the little lakeside village of Rorsbach to which they had fled right across Switzerland that morning, as soon as the German papers had reported the finding of the murdered policeman. Cain could guess who had helped the Swiss Police on that one!

Jim lit yet another cigarette, and Cain noticed his fingers trembled slightly as he did so. Obviously the double agent was pretty shaky, and he knew why. Jim wanted to have the thing done with so that he could close down his station and get out of the country. 'What about the Jerry girl?' he inquired.

'You mean whether they'll find her or not before you can pack up?'

'Yes.' The music was reverberating back and forth across the big Lake now and Cain could see the gleam of the instruments, as the procession began to stream out of the village.

'I don't know, Foote, except that she's proved herself pretty resourceful up to now. According to what I gathered from Pink-face she seems to have gone to ground in Munich. It's a big city and as a German she'll know the ropes. But I don't think she can survive long without other papers, money, ration cards and the like, if the Gestapo starts bearing down in strength.' He paused, his brow creased in a frown, as they started to come level with the procession, 'That is, if she really *did* go to Munich.'

'What do you mean?'

But Cain never managed to answer the question, for in an instant they were swamped by the crazy, colourful, shrieking procession: grotesquely masked witches in ragged sackcloth dresses, armed with brooms; huge bulbous-headed horrors with the painted faces of idiots, swinging wooden rattles and throwing cheap caramels to the screaming children who were everywhere under foot; brawny, sweating young men in the multi-coloured costumes of medieval pages, waving great red and white Swiss flags; and the musicians, dressed as skeletons, marching with a strange, stiff-legged step, and rigid bodies. 'What in all hell's name is this?' Cain roared, cupping his hand around his mouth and neatly avoiding a kiss from a brawny woman with breasts like balloons under her skimpy costume.

'*Fastnacht.* Tomorrow is what they call Rose Monday. They're working up to a climax,' Foote yelled.

'So I see,' Cain commented drily, as one of the witches, who were obviously costumed men, made an obscene thrust with his broom at the lower regions of a fat blonde, dressed in a ballet skirt and black net stockings. The crowd roared with laughter as the blonde clasped the assaulted area and yelled, with an expression of mock pain on her fat face.

'It's an old fertility rite,' Jim lowered his voice as the procession began to move off. 'They've always celebrated it right along the border area from Cologne to Munich, and through Eastern Belgium, Switzerland and Austria too. It starts on the eleventh hour of the eleventh day of the eleventh month of the year, but really gets going this weekend. On Ash Wednesday, it's all over.' He lit another cigarette and grinned as a couple of men passed by in a hurry, trying to catch up with the rest, one dressed as a woman with enormous breasts, pushing the other, disguised as a baby, complete with bonnet and bottle, in an ancient, buckled-wheeled pram. 'It's not bad if you're out for a little bit of slap-and-tickle. Even the Swiss women can let their hair down at this time of the year – with the help of a lot of schnapps and beer, of course.'

'Of course!'

They walked on in silence for a little while longer. Soon Jim would have to turn and catch the bus back to St Gallen. Cain didn't want the others, waiting for him in the lakeside *pension,* to see the double agent; they might start asking awkward questions. They approached a neat line of boats, partially hidden by drying nets, each locked to a stake in the careful Swiss fashion and guarded by a young soldier in the ill-fitting grey uniform of the Federal Territorials, a carbine slung carelessly over his bent shoulder. 'What's the guard in aid of?' Cain asked thoughtfully.

Foote explained. 'This was a pretty popular tourist resort before the war. But that died a natural death in 1939, so the local fishermen started to do a bit of smuggling – across the water,' he indicated the faint smudge which was Friedrichshafen. 'Coffee, butter, cigarettes and the like. And being good businessmen like all Swiss,' again Foote did not conceal his contempt for his host nation, 'they reasoned, that they shouldn't bring back their boats empty. So they started a nice little thriving business in Jerry deserters and civvies who wanted to get out of the place. That was until May 1940 and the Jerries began to show their strength. The Swiss saw the writing on the wall. Hell, if anybody's going to survive this war by hook or by crook it's going to be them, you can be sure.'

Cain ignored Foote's cynicism at the expense of the Swiss. 'Get on with it,' he urged.

'So, with their usual eye to the main chance, once the Nazis had knocked hell out of the froggies, they promised that there'd be no more smuggling *in* or *out* of Germany. That's why that poor bored squaddie's standing there like the proverbial spare penis at a wedding. It's his job to check the fishermen when they go out to fish and once again when they return.'

'I see,' Cain said slowly. 'Listen, Foote, how far do you think Germany is from here?'

'Well, Friedrichshafen is about five or six miles, but of course, Jerry territorial waters start two miles out. Why do you ask, Cain?'

Cain smiled softly. 'I thought I might pay a little visit to the Reich again. It's been a good half year since I was last there, you know.'

Foote stopped in mid-stride and looked at him as if he had suddenly gone crazy. 'You're kidding, aren't you?' he demanded.

'No.'

'But Cain, you wouldn't even get past the border checkpoint.'

'But what if I didn't cross at one of the approved points, Foote?'

'You mean the boats?'

'Yes.'

Foote steered him round firmly and said, 'Just have another gander at them, man. They're locked up, guarded day and night and look at those arc-lights. Even though the Jerries are always pressing for a blackout at this side of the Lake so that the lights don't guide the RAF to Friedrichshafen, they keep those arc-lights on all night. Cain, it would be almost impossible to nobble that sentry at night without him being able to raise the alarm. Okay, so you make it and you manage to get a boat,' he continued in exasperation, 'you'd have to face the Jerry boat patrols – they're always out there at night. Then what do you propose to do on the other side, if you get that far, without any kind of papers? Cain, it would be absolute, sheer bloody suicide!'

'Yes, I suppose you're right, Foote,' Cain answered slowly, but there was no conviction in his voice.

'Gentlemen,' Cain said formally, 'I'm going to make you a proposition.'

'We're in trouble,' Spiv sighed. 'When officers start calling ORs gents, they're always for the high jump.'

None of the others, grouped around the scrubbed wooden table in the little room with its view across the Lake, laughed at Spiv's sally. They were all too tense. They knew it would not be long before the Swiss police traced their flight from Geneva to the little lakeside village.

'All right,' Cain continued, raising his voice above the noise of fireworks, being let off by the celebrating throng outside in the cobbled street, 'you all know that we're in a pretty dicey situation. Soon the Swiss heavies will be breathing down our necks. At present France is out of the question, though I have asked our people at the Embassy in Berne, to contact HQ to see whether in due course they can get a Lysander into the French Jura to pick us up. But that'll take days. So,' he hesitated for a fraction of a second, 'there's only one other place left–'

'–Germany?' Abel said the word for him.

'Yes.'

'Christ!' Spiv exclaimed. 'Hand me a razor blade somebody and I'll commit suicide straight off!'

Cain ignored the comment, though he knew how justified it was. 'For reasons I can't go into here, I must find that blonde and make damn sure she doesn't tell the Gestapo what she knows.' He hurried on before anyone could ask an awkward question. 'You see I don't think she went to Munich as that German Pink-face believed.'

'How do you mean, Cain?' Mac asked.

'Well, look at it like this. We've seen that she's a very resourceful girl. Would a girl like

148

that leave such an obvious trail, unless she intended that it should be obvious?'

'A red herring?' Abel asked.

'Yes.'

'But if she's not in Munich, where might she be?'

'Now that I don't know. She's got her passport, but she'll want to replace that soon with new ID and she's got to eat – and she can't do that either for too long without a ration book. In short, she needs a new identity. Obviously she wouldn't stay in a small place while she gets it.'

'Yeah,' Abel agreed. 'A good-looker like she is, according to Spiv here, and a stranger too, would stand out in a village.'

'So, it's got to be a larger place and there are only two on the German side of the Lake – Schaffhausen or Friedrichshafen. And reasoning that she wouldn't want to travel much, in case of being asked for ID, it's my guess, but only a guess, that she's gone to ground in Friedrichshafen itself.'

'There are one or two little defects in your logic, skipper,' Abel mused, 'but I'll buy it.' He smiled suddenly. 'And I'm with you.'

'Thanks, Abel,' Cain breathed out a sigh of relief, and began to explain his plan for stealing a boat and crossing the Lake.

Spiv was not so easily convinced as the American, however. When Cain had finished, he leaned back in the high-backed, carved wooden chair and sucked his teeth thoughtfully. Outside the noise was reaching a crescendo. Someone was banging a big drum, as if he intended to burst the skin.

'But if the place is as well-lit at night, as you say, sir, how are we gonna get close enough to grab the sentry without him hollering his head off? That's problem number one – and I've got plenty more where that one comes from!' he added grimly.

Cain smiled. 'One minute.' He rose and walked to the big, hand-painted rustic wardrobe in the corner and opened it with his hook. He bent swiftly and slipped the nearest domed-head over his own and turned to face them.

'Hell's bells,' Spiv exclaimed, 'it's bloody old Frankenstein himself!'

'Not exactly,' Cain's voice, muffled slightly by the hideous mask with its nut-cracker jaws and nose, and the jet-black, glaring, frightening wild eyes, explained. 'I'm supposed to be so hideous as to frighten off evil spirits. It's an old Swiss custom at this time of the year.'

'Well, it ruddy well frightens me all right,' Spiv admitted.

'I hope it doesn't do the same with our tame sentry,' Cain answered, tugging the mask off, 'because this is the way we're going to get close to him without any fuss and feathers...'

THREE

Rorsbach had gone crazy, absolutely crazy!

The clash of cymbals, the thud-thud of the big drums, the brazen blare of the brass echoed and re-echoed down the narrow cobbled lakeside streets, filled with laughing, shrieking, drunken men, women, and children, all costumed and firing their cap guns into the night air, adding to the impossible racket.

Determinedly the four grotesquely masked figures pushed their way through the excited throng. The lead was taken by one with the mask of a Victorian Punch. Number two had the face of Snow White's Dopey, the crazy face of a Swiss mountain farmer, the result of 1,000 years of in-breeding. The third member of the quartet was the Devil himself, all glaring eyes and fiercely bared teeth. Number four was the Lecher, with thick red, sensual lips, cynical eyes and his long stiff *papier-mâché* nose thrust straight upwards, an all-too obvious phallic symbol.

A coarse-faced drunken woman in a low-cut peasant blouse, barred their way, and giggling furiously, grabbed at the Lecher's nose. The Lecher pushed her away and the sticky tape which held her breasts up to give her a deep cleavage snapped. Her breasts fell down to her stomach and she started to sob, leaning against a wall. A tall man in the costume of a harlequin stepped up to her and began to undo her blouse buttons, at which she started to giggle again.

'*Besoffene Sau!*' the Lecher growled and pushed back a fat man facing the wall urinating with his free hand, eating a sausage sandwich with the other. A small green balloon floated from his battered straw hat. As an afterthought seemingly, the Lecher pressed the glowing end of his cheap cigar against the balloon. It exploded with a slight plop.

'Oops, pardon me!' the man facing the wall said thickly. 'It must have just slipped out!'

'Then slip it back in again,' the Lecher said in a thick Cockney accent. And then finally, free of the crowd, the Ultra team was moving down the lakeside path in a drunken, swaying gait.

The sentry loomed up out of the hectic darkness. He was clearly outlined in the glaring white light of the arcs suspended above the boats he was guarding.

A fat, middle-aged territorial, a rifle slung carelessly over his shoulder, leaned against a post clearly bored, wishing that he could be taking part in the festivities.

'Okay, *now!*' Punch said, when they were about ten yards away from him.

Dopey pulled the bottle of fiery Swiss plum brandy from his pocket and broke into a shambling drunken run, singing at the top of his voice in a thick, intoxicated caterwaul. *'Heute blau ... morgen blau ... und ubermorgen wieder...'* The fat sentry grinned and smacked his thick lips in anticipation. Perhaps he might get a free drink after all.

The others staggered after their breakaway friend, yelling, 'bring back the bottle ... hey, bring back that shitty bottle!' But Dopey was not listening. He was obviously filled with the milk of human kindness, the desire to give. Zig-zagging violently, he reached the sentry and proffered the bottle. 'Poor shit-chap,' he said thickly. 'On stag on a night like this ... here, put a shot of this behind yer collar, pal.'

Eagerly the fat sentry reached for the bottle before the drunk's pals caught up with him. At that moment, the Devil bent down. There was the silver gleam of metal clippers in the glaring white light.

The lights went out suddenly.

'Eh, what–'

The sentry's alarmed voice died abruptly in the thick, sudden darkness. There was the sound of a body falling on the concrete.

Five minutes later they had cut through the chain holding the nearest boat, checked that its tank was full of petrol and were pushing it out into the shallows, the little noise they made drowned by the racket from the village. After ten minutes when they were fifty yards or more from the shore, they dared to start the outboard motor. It fired instantly. They were on their way.

'*Halt! Wer da!*' the harsh metallic command echoed across the still water from the loudhailer.

'*Rozzers!*' Spiv cried. '*Jerry rozzers!*'

Up ahead they could see the lean sharp outline of another motor boat.

'*Halt! Wasserschutzpolizei hier,*' the harsh voice ordered once more. A searchlight flicked on.

'Kraut water police,' Spiv said hastily.

As the bright white beam started to swing across the dark water towards them, Cain reacted. 'Get those masks on – quick. Abel get hold of that bottle! We're Swiss drunks, okay?'

'Roger, skipper!'

With frenzied fumbling, they slipped on the domed masks, just as the searchlight came to rest on the little boat and exposed them to the German patrol.

The German boat came alongside wearily. Mac, fumbling for his device, caught a glimpse of a man crouched behind the twin Spandaus mounted on the deck, and another man at the wheel. The space behind him where the engines were was empty.

'What are you doing out here at this time of night?' The man at the wheel called, in a voice which was obviously used to giving orders – and having them carried out. 'You're just about to enter German territorial waters.' He brought the long lean motor boat closer to the fishing boat so that he could see its occupants more clearly.

Abel rose to his feet drunkenly and nearly toppled overboard. 'We're celebrating Carnival, my friend,' he cried, slurring his words. 'Here have a drink, General!'

He thrust the bottle towards the policeman and nearly fell overboard again.

'Watch it, you stupid Swiss cheese-head,' the man at the wheel said in alarm. 'You were nearly over the side then.'

'Don't matter … don't matter,' Abel said. 'The Lake's full of schnapps tonight, General.'

Behind him, Mac slipped his device over the side of the German boat.

'Not as full as you are at the moment,' the German said, half-amused, half-disgusted at the drunken Swiss. 'All right, now, get yourself back the way you've come, or the damned lot of you will find yourselves in serious trouble. Off with you now – and don't let me find you here again tonight. *Heil Hitler!*'

'Heil bloody Hitler!' Spiv grumbled beneath his breath as the German opened the throttle and with its sharp prow rising steeply into the air, the German craft raced away, the twin jets of wild white water at its rear rocking their own boat violently. 'That's torn it, sir. Now what are we soddingly well gonna do?'

'I don't know, Spiv,' Cain said, realizing – though he hated to admit it even to himself – that his plan to cross the Lake had failed miserably, 'I don't bloody well know.'

'Dinna fash yersen,' Mac said, breaking the gloomy silence of the others. 'Yon Jerries won't get far this night.'

They swung round on him. 'Why?'

'On account of the fact I gave them a little present to take with them.'

'A present?' Cain demanded impatiently, 'what are you getting at, Mac?'

'You remember the wee bomb I made for that German lassie?'

'You don't mean you've planted it on them?' Cain cut in excitedly, hardly daring to believe his ears.

'Ay. I'll give 'em about ten minutes.'

'Well, come on,' Cain cried, 'let's get going!'

Hurriedly, Abel started the motor again. Swiftly they swung the boat round and started heading for the German side of the Lake once more, heads twisted to the east,

156

waiting expectantly for the explosion that would tell them Mac's scheme had worked; or the angry command, followed by the high-pitched burr of the twin Spandaus which would indicate it hadn't.

Now they could see the faint pink glare of Friedrichshafen's factories in the sky ahead, which no amount of blackout devices could completely cut out.

But Mac's skill did not fail them. Precisely ten minutes after the German boat had left them, there was a dull thump across the water, followed an instant later by a bright sheet of scarlet flame.

'Wow!' Abel yelled exuberantly, 'you pulled it off, you Scots wizard you!'

'Ay, it was no bad,' Mac admitted modestly, 'if I do say so mysen.'

Thirty minutes later, the little boat hit the other bank. The Ultra team was in Nazi Germany once again.

FOUR

'It's not a bad haul really, Colleague Pannwitz,' the elderly Munich Police Lieutenant said hopefully. Pannwitz dropped the typed list to the floor of Munich's *Polizei Prasidiums* main office. 'Fourteen deserters from the

Wehrmacht, ten black marketeers and pimps, three escaped Ivan POWs and one half-Jew,' he recited the list, which was the result of the great raid that day. 'But no damned blonde! Where in God's name is the bitch?'

The Police Lieutenant shrugged helplessly. 'We searched every known hangout for such people on the run, Colleague Pannwitz – cheap hotels, soldiers' homes, the foreign labourers' barracks, whore-houses – even the Station Mission for Lonely Girls. Everywhere!' Pannwitz said nothing, so he continued. 'Of course, it could be that she isn't in Munich in the first place.'

'Of course, she is in Munich, man!' Pannwitz cried, his pink face flushing a deeper red with anger. 'She bought a third class ticket from Friedrichshafen for Munich, didn't she?'

'The fact she bought a ticket doesn't mean she used it, Colleague Pannwitz,' the Police Lieutenant said softly.

Pannwitz bit back an angry rejoinder just in time, and to cover up his confusion and rage, he strode over to the window and stared out at the gloomy panorama of a wartime German morning. The shabby civilians, pale-faced, bent-shouldered and undernourished; the soldiers sturdy, but with that same defeated look in their eyes, the knowledge that they were just cannon-fodder, destined sooner or later to be consumed by the greedy maws of that terrible beast, the war in the East.

But the sight did not depress Pannwitz. Instead it filled him with an even greater sense of urgency to find the girl and root out the traitors in Germany who were betraying those people down there to the Russian spies. Of course, the old crock of a cop behind him was right. The purchase of the ticket proved nothing. He swung round, a fake smile on his face, his anger conquered. '*Naturlich, Herr Kollege,* you are right,' he said with false bonhomie. 'A good policeman should never assume anything. All that must concern him is fact – hard facts. Mueller always says that. Like me he was a cop before they came along.'

The Lieutenant chuckled; he knew who *they* were. 'I know, I know. I remember the days when your Gestapo Mueller thought it was a lot to give forty pfennigs' monthly subscription to the Party funds.'

Pannwitz chuckled too, though he had never felt less like laughing in his life. But he needed the old cop's co-operation: two heads were better than one. 'Yes, he's as tight as a Yid that one. But that's neither here nor there. If I don't find that girl soon, Mueller will have my arse. Now if she didn't come to Munich, where did she go?'

'There are plenty of little places between here and Friedrichshafen,' the Lieutenant suggested. 'And the train did stop three times.'

'Completely out of the question! The girl was on the run for two years before the Gestapo picked her up. She knows the ropes. She'd stick out like a sore thumb in a small place.' Abruptly Pannwitz had an idea. 'The Friedrichshafen–Munich train that she took – *if* she took it – where is it now?'

'Most of it went on to Poland, and from there to Russia.'

'*Ach, Scheisse!*' Pannwitz cursed. 'All right, then, contact every little place between here and Friedrichshafen, the ones where the train stopped, and check whether anyone was spotted getting off there.'

'I thought you might ask me that, Colleague Pannwitz, and I've already checked. She didn't get off at any of the three stations that come into question. However, we could appeal to the public over the radio to come forward if they have seen her?'

Pannwitz shook his head. 'No, that would take too much time – and time we don't have.'

'There is one carriage left at Munich's shunting station still,' the old cop said.

'What?'

'Yes, the usual compartment for severely wounded and the two for nursing mothers.' He grinned. 'The railway authorities unhooked that one from the troop train at

160

Munich, naturally. There'll be no nursing mothers where the boys are going and what delayed action charges they have left behind them won't explode yet for another nine months, eh?'

Pannwitz was in no mood for humour. 'Come on,' he said urgently, 'let's go and have a look at the damned thing. It might tell us something.'

As the Police Lieutenant took up his high-peaked hat, he told himself with amusement that Colleague Pannwitz was down to clutching at straws.

Nearly a hundred miles away at Friedrich-shafen, Cain followed the tram line into the centre of the industrial city – it was an old trick for finding the way. He was wondering exactly the same thing at that moment. What proof did he have that she had gone to ground here? None, a little voice at the back of his brain said, 'absolutely none'. But he ignored the voice and trudged on with the rest. They were now entering the centre. Ruined houses were everywhere, their interiors, once intimate and domestic, exposed now to the lack-lustre gaze of the passers-by. They turned a corner and saw the station in front of them. Beyond it lay the goods yard, a mess of smashed, rusting locomotives and shattered coaches, some of them rearing high in the air like horses.

'This is as good a place as any to take a load off our plates o' meat, sir,' Spiv whispered, 'and have a dekko at what the form is.'

Cain nodded agreement. Usually German stations were surrounded by cheap little cafés and hotels which in wartime were filled with foreigners of all nationalities (after all there were nine million foreign workers in the Reich) where no questions would be asked. 'Over there,' he snapped, *'Zum Weissl Rossl.'* Obediently they trooped into the smoky, dingy café, whose door bore the legend, *'Wir grussen hier mit Heil Hitler'.*

'Cor blimey,' Spiv scoffed, 'fancy having to say God Bless the King every time you entered a boozer.'

'Shut up,' Cain hissed and started to thread his way through the tables, towards an empty alcove in the corner.

Abel ordered coffee and the *Stamm,* the only meal on the pathetic hand-written menu for which they didn't need ration coupons. The slipper-clad, sloppy owner brought the ersatz coffee, supplied with a small envelope of saccharine, and four bowls of the *Stamm,* which was pea soup.

Spiv looked at it while the owner shuffled back to the game of *skat* going on near the door. 'The only meat this bloody soup ever saw was that bloke's thumb in it, just now.'

But surprisingly enough the soup, meat-less as it was, tasted good, and they ate it in

162

silence, realizing for the first time, just how hungry they were.

Over the bitter substitute coffee, Cain explained what he intended doing with more confidence than he felt. 'Listen, the first thing is find somewhere to get our heads down for the night – somewhere where they won't ask for papers.'

'A knocking shop?' Spiv suggested.

'No, too dangerous. I bet these days there are always military police patrols checking brothels out for deserters.'

'What about this place? The sign outside said rooms,' Abel said. 'I'll go and see what I can do, if you like. That guy over there,' he indicated the proprietor, 'doesn't look to me like a feller who would be averse to a little persuasion.' He made the continental gesture of counting money.

Out of the corner of their eyes, they watched as Abel took the man to one side and whispered in his ear. The man nodded a couple of times and looked pointedly in their direction once; then notes of the realm changed hands furtively and a smiling Abel came walking back to their table. 'Two nights and no questions asked,' he said softly. 'That man's got a heart as big as his pocket book.'

'What did you tell him?' Cain asked.

'We're foreign workers, sent here from Berlin. Our factory was bombed. We lost everything and we're to wait here until the authorities fix us up with new papers and a new job.' He winked at them. 'From the goodness of his heart, he'll even supply us with an evening meal.'

'How much?' Spiv asked.

'Five marks a head.'

'The bloody cut-throat! He should have joined the Sal Val – he's so generous.'

'All right,' Cain broke in hastily. 'We're fixed up here for the next forty-eight hours, it seems. Now we pray we can find the blonde fast.'

'*Pray* is the operative word, sir,' Spiv said and for once there was no humour in his cockney voice.

That same evening Pannwitz found the hat in the 'badly-injured' compartment, while the Lieutenant and the curious blue-uniformed railway policemen looked on. 'It's hers,' he proclaimed in triumph, dragging it from beneath the seat.

'Are you sure, Colleague Pannwitz? It's a very ordinary looking hat.'

'Of course I'm sure. Look at the label inside – here. *Bon Marché Genéve*. She must have bought it while we were there – with our good money, the Yiddish bitch!'

'So that means,' the other man summed up, 'that she did come to Munich after all. But why did she throw away a perfectly good hat like that? Clothes don't grow on trees in Germany these days, do they?'

The question stumped Pannwitz for a moment. Then he dismissed the hat and took another tack, thinking aloud. 'But what would she be doing travelling in a reserved compartment like this? The guard would certainly have spotted her and ordered her out some time during the journey to Munich.'

'Yes, we're very strict about that, *Kommissar*,' the senior railway policeman said. 'Orders from above. God knows there are enough wounded in Germany nowadays.'

'Yes, yes,' Pannwitz said absently, trying to puzzle it all out. Obviously the woman had boarded the train after all at Friedrichshafen – the hat proved that. And she had not been traced to any of the three stops between there and Munich. So what had happened to her on the train?

'Yes,' the Lieutenant said slowly, enjoying the look of bewilderment on the Gestapo man's pink face, 'it almost looks as if your Jewess has disappeared into thin air, doesn't it, dear colleague?'

'*Scheisse!*' was *Oberkommissar* Heinz Pannwitz's sole response.

FIVE

It was a strange raid.

The British usually preferred to attack at night. Today they were coming in daylight, picked up by German radar as soon as they crossed the French coast at Dunkirk. *Luftwaffe* HQ scrambled its fighter wing at Laon, but by the time they were airborne, the seventy odd, four-engine Lancasters had disappeared into a sudden snow storm.

German radar picked them up again thirty minutes later, just as they were passing over the French Jura and climbing slowly, not only because they were flying over the mountains, but because they were going to pass over neutral Switzerland. Naturally the Swiss flak opened up at them, but their ill-trained territorial gunners were not accurate and eventually the officer responsible for frontier flak ordered a cease-fire. As he explained cynically to his second-in-command: 'We'll send the British a diplomatic note of protest. It might be more effective than those oafs of farmboys on the guns!'

By now, the whole of Southern Germany was on alarm stage three, and in the underground plotting room of Air Defence

Command South, the experts were desperately trying to work out what the British target would be. Schweinefurt and the ball bearing plants once again? Or Augsburg with its tank plants? Perhaps even Munich, though that was about the limit of their range.

But all their guesses were wrong. The RAF was making this an easy one. First the storm over Northern France, which the Air Ministry's Met Section had confidently predicted would cover them against the German fighters; then the flight over neutral Switzerland; now the closest target of all in Southern Germany – Friedrichshafen!

Rosamund Hirsch was spending the afternoon in the cinema – it was warm and no one asked questions there – when the film suddenly went dead. Abruptly the lights went on and the manager was bellowing from the stage. 'Air raid ... air raid! Everyone to the nearest shelter!'

To the accompaniment of 'We March Against England' being played by a military band over the cracked loudspeaker, the mixed crowd of civilians and soldiers hurried out to the shelters. It was the moment that the girl had been waiting desperately for, for the last two days and she seized the opportunity offered her eagerly. Sheltering in a doorway, ducking inside every time a warden ran by or a patrol of Hitler Youth firewatchers, armed with stirrup pumps, doubled past, she watched and waited.

Bomb after bomb came whistling down. She ducked automatically and opened her mouth to prevent her eardrums from being burst by their detonation. All around, the walls of the office buildings shook and trembled violently. Hot waves of acrid air struck her in the face time and time again. A man ran by screaming, his clothes on fire, a piece of white phosphorous embedded in his face burning cruelly. A woman followed, pushing a pram containing a child's corpse. The girl shuddered and covered her face with her trembling hands to blot out the sight. She knew she must not leave her watching place. She must stick it out!

Finally it was over. The Lancasters swung away to the west, leaving the stricken city behind them, heading for their fields in East Anglia and the bacon and eggs that would be waiting for them, heedless of the misery they left behind them.

After all, this was total war.

As the thin wail of the siren sounding the all-clear started to fill the still echoing sky, Rosamund Hirsch ventured out into a burning, completely transformed Friedrichshafen. She staggered over the rubble, past a smouldering, completely burnt-out car, its occupants already shrivelled mummified black pigmies. Further on, in the gutter lay something resembling a tennis ball. It was a baby's head! She recoiled with horror as a clay-faced warden came stumbling out of the wrecked house, bearing a pail. 'The rest of it is in here,' he said thickly and passed on.

Blindly she staggered on.

And then Rosamund Hirsch found what she was seeking. A still burning workers' high tenement being hosed by soot-blackened firemen, soaked to the waist by water, their faces exhausted, while others hacked away desperately at the entrance to the cellar air-raid shelter. 'What happened?' she asked a blank-eyed woman, with a bloody bandage round her head, seemingly unaware that she was naked to the waist. 'Trapped ... trapped ... all of them trapped in the cellar,' the woman answered, her voice toneless. *'My baby...'*

Rosamund Hirsch left her and ran across the debris-littered street to the door. By the red glare of the flames, she could read the list of names easily. Her eyes flew down them. *Hoffnung* the name seemed to leap up at her. That was it! It seemed like a symbol to her at that moment.

'Hey, you, get away there!' an angry voice cried. 'Get away there. This thing's likely to come down at any moment!'

She swung round. A fat, middle-aged policeman in a steel helmet was glaring at her, his face lathered in sweat. 'Clear out, or you'll get yourself killed!'

She moved away quickly, so that he couldn't see the little smile of triumph on her face. *She had it!*

It was Spiv who spotted her – naturally. They had not dared to take cover during the raid, in case an air raid warden or other official present in the shelter asked them awkward questions. Now they were moving back to their hotel, shifting a bit of rubble at a still smoking ruin and then moving on to the next, as if they were helping the rescue workers who were hacking at the rubble, looking for survivors. Once they avoided a police patrol, watching for looters, by carrying away a couple of dead women to the collecting point at the bottom of the street, where the dead were piled up on one another like logs of wood.

They had just turned a corner, and moved past a burnt-out fire-engine, its dead crew, still in position, as if they were ready to spring into action at any moment. Suddenly Spiv exclaimed, 'It's her, sir.'

'Who?'

'The blonde – the Jerry bint we're looking for!'

Cain forgot the horror all around them. 'Where?' he rapped urgently.

'Up there – just going through that passage.'

Cain saw a tall, slim blonde with pretty legs walking through the smoke some fifty yards away. 'You're sure?'

'Of course I am, sir.'

'Then come on.'

They dropped their previous caution and sprinted down the debris-littered street after her. A black-faced, bare-headed soldier shouted at them angrily. They ignored him, too intent on the girl. They caught up with her, just before she emerged from the passage into the main street, filled with officials and refugees from the ruins.

'What now, sir?' Spiv asked swiftly.

'Act first, explain later... Abel, Mac, you watch our rear. Okay, here we go.'

Cain burst forward. His good hand shot over her mouth before she could scream. He dug his hook into the small of her back so that she would think it was a gun and hissed, 'Don't be afraid, we're friends!'

Behind him Mac and Abel had kicked open the half-shattered door of a smoking ruin, the noise they made covered by the sudden wail of an ambulance siren. Hastily Cain steered her towards it, his hand still clasped over her mouth. He shoved her through into the brick-rubble and plaster mess of what had once been a kitchen and pushed her against the wall. To his rear, the other three were hastily piling fallen timbers and bits of wreckage against the inside of the door, as a primitive barricade against unwelcome visitors.

Cain waited till they were finished, then he said, 'I'll let you go now, if you promise not to scream. Nod your head if you agree.'

She nodded.

Slowly he released the pressure of his hand on her mouth. She swung round swiftly to face him, her face determined, but her eyes full of fear. 'Who are you?' she demanded, ready to play the role of her life – the outraged innocent – if what she feared, turned out to be true. Now she was fighting for her life and she knew she had the emergency documents in her pocket to back up her statements.

'Englishmen.'

'Englishmen!' she exclaimed. 'What, escaped prisoners-of-war?'

Cain shook his head, saying nothing for the moment, letting her talk and attempting to assess her quickly.

'What are Englishmen doing here?' she cried. 'Are you spies? I don't understand.'

'You don't need to understand,' Cain said gently. 'All you need to know is that we have come here to help you.'

The fear fled from her eyes to be replaced by a new look of hope. 'Help me?'

'Yes, Miss Hirsch. I can't tell you very much. All I can tell you is that we shall be taking you back to Switzerland tonight as

172

soon as it gets dark. From there we'll be moving to another country in a few days' time, where an aeroplane will be waiting for us to take us back to England. Don't ask me why England – or you other three either.' He flung a glance at the others who were staring at him curiously, obviously wondering why the girl had to be taken to England; she would have been safe enough in Switzerland.

'There is one reason I cannot leave,' the blonde's eyes fell, 'my mother!'

'How do you mean?' Cain asked swiftly.

She explained how the Gestapo had blackmailed her into helping them.

Cain smiled encouragingly when she was finished. 'But don't you see, Miss Hirsch? Once we have managed to get you out of here, you will have vanished. Nobody on their side will know whether you're dead or alive and as long as they don't know, they're going to keep your mother alive as a potential hostage.'

'Of course,' she breathed gratefully. 'You're right.' She smiled in a way she had not smiled for years. 'Yes, I shall come with you to England.'

'Well done,' Cain said approvingly. 'Then let's get the devil out of here before some nosey policeman starts knocking on the door.'

One hour later they were safely hidden in

an abandoned summer house, overlooking the road to the Lake. In five hours it would be dark and they could safely set out with the boat for the Swiss side.

SIX

The afternoon dragged by in heavy silence, broken only by the muted chug-chug of the odd wood-burning truck or the rattle of an ox-drawn farm cart. The others slept while Abel kept guard near the second floor window overlooking the track to the Lake, chatting softly to the girl who was too nervous and excited to sleep.

She told him what it had been like to be on the run as a Jewess; how she had been terrified to sleep in a room with another of the female entertainers, in case she might talk in her sleep; how sometimes she had been forced to spend whole nights simply walking and smoking. She told him how the women in Dachau, who could stand the horror of the camp no longer, would break off slivers of enamel from the inside of the latrine buckets and slit their wrists under the cover of their blankets during the night, praying to be allowed to die without being discovered.

'For three years I've had that kind of a life,' she said softly. 'Always on my guard. Never being able to relax. Always playing a role from the first thing in the morning to the last at night, even in my sleep. A Jewish ghost in an Aryan world. And now it's nearly all over.' She smiled suddenly at him. 'I know it's a cliché, but it's like having a great, heavy weight removed from one's shoulders.'

Impulsively Abel put out his hand and patted hers. 'Don't worry any more. We'll look after you. You're in good hands.'

Her smile widened. 'I haven't the faintest idea into whose hands I've fallen, but I trust you all right. England,' she mused a little later, after they had ducked to let an old man in the blue apron of a fisherman go cycling rapidly by, 'I wonder what it'll be like. I've always visualized Englishmen as tall and thin with moustaches – like Mr Chamberlain. But your comrades, they don't look like that.'

'That they don't,' Abel agreed. 'The English – they're a very hard, cynical, realistic people who when they know what they want, go after it, regardless of the cost.'

The girl looked at him curiously. 'You don't like them, do you?'

'Not much, but those men down there are good comrades. We all stick together. I guess because we have to – we need each other.

175

Besides,' he smiled suddenly, 'there are other places you can go to one day, you know.'

'For instance?'

'America.'

'*America?*' She looked at him and realized that for the first time she was looking at a man, not as a potential enemy, but as a possible friend or lover. Instinctively she patted his hand. 'We'll see,' she said, using the formula women all over the world use on such occasions, 'we'll see.'

'Of course. First we've got to get across that Lake and through Switzerland.'

At 5.00 pm Abel wakened the others and they ate the boiled maize cobs which the girl had discovered hanging from the previous summer, under the cottage's eaves, washing the unpalatable corn down with a slug each from Spiv's flask of schnapps. Then Cain explained to them what they were going to do.

'We can assume that there might be some sort of patrol along the bank of the Lake, even if it consists of the local bobby for this part of Friedrichshafen. Okay, we'll move towards the boat as soon as it gets dark. Then if we are spotted before we get to it, we can always appear to be ordinary folk going about their normal business. Having an evening stroll before turning in, that sort of thing. Now you Abel, our best German speaker, and you Miss Hirsch, will take the lead. We'll follow at a distance just in case you bump into trouble. The two of you, Abel, can act as a courting couple–'

'Sodding hell,' Spiv interrupted in mock indignation. 'Can yer beat it? It's allus the officers and gents who get the best jobs!'

'And you'll get a bang on the head, if you don't shut up, Spiv,' Cain said firmly, but with a grin on his face. He felt in a good mood. The mission had been successful and once they were across the Lake, he didn't think they would have much trouble in Switzerland. He'd worry about France later. 'This time we can't risk starting the motor until we're out of Jerry waters, so this time we'll have to paddle the first couple of miles. So the lot of you had better scout around this place and see what you can find that might serve as a paddle.' He glanced swiftly at his watch. 'We leave in exactly thirty-five minutes. All right, get on with it.'

Soft-footed, they padded down the track behind the dim outline of Abel and the girl, some fifty yards ahead. Each one of them carried a plate to paddle with in one hand, but the other was clutched around the butt of the pistol hidden in his pocket. The place where the boat was hidden was only a couple of hundred yards away; they were taking no chances now.

Since they left the house they had not seen a soul. Perhaps the raid that morning had frightened the civilians off the streets, Cain told himself. All the same, he was taking no chances. If they were spotted by a patrol with a boat which was obviously Swiss, it would be no use attempting explanations. They would have to fight it out. It would be shoot and run.

Abel and the girl were a hundred yards away from the boat now. They stopped and embraced each other, as Cain had ordered to give them a good opportunity to check whether all was clear.

'He's on a bloody good thing,' Spiv said enviously.

Cain wasn't listening. He was concentrating on the couple. They started to stroll on again, and breathed out a sigh of relief.

Nobody in sight.

'Okay, Spiv,' he ordered, 'off you go!'

Clutching his pot plate close to his side, Spiv doubled into the trees to their left, which fringed the boat's hiding place.

'Now you, Mac!'

The burly Scot followed. Cain posted himself in the deeper shadow cast by the trees, pistol clenched in his fist. A hundred yards away, Abel and the girl were embracing again, keeping a look-out for any danger from that quarter.

A shrill whistle cut the night silence.

178

Once, twice, three times. It was the signal!

Abel and the girl broke away from each other, as if surprised by an enraged father, and began running through the trees. Cain did the same, not caring now, how much noise he made as he blundered through the tight firs. He burst through the last of them and stopped short.

The others were gathered on the bank, faces heavy with shock, bodies rigid.

'What's the matter?' he gasped.

Spiv held up the end of the rope with which they had secured the boat to the bank. 'Somebody's nicked the sodding boat, sir,' he said.

'Oh Christ!' Cain groaned. The plate dropped from beneath his arm and shattered to a thousand pieces on the ground at his feet.

They were trapped in Nazi Germany!

THE JOURNEY HOME

'The greatest adventure of all is the adventure of taking one's life into one's own hands and depending on one's own resources.'

Eric Williams.

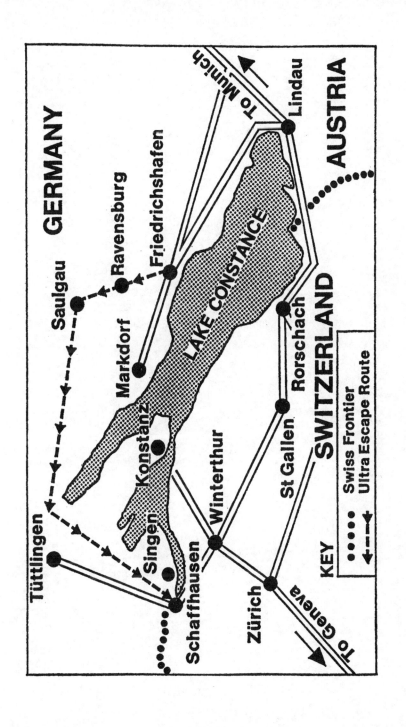

GERMANY

AUSTRIA

To Munich

Lindau

Ravensburg

Saulgau

Friedrichshafen

Markdorf

LAKE CONSTANCE

Rorschach

Konstanz

SWITZERLAND

Winterthur

St Gallen

Singen

Tüttlingen

Schaffhausen

Zürich

To Geneva

KEY

Swiss Frontier

Ultra Escape Route

ONE

'*Ja, bitte?*' Pannwitz snapped.

The voice on the other end of the line was clearly very excited. '*Herr Oberkommissar,* we've found a boat!'

'How very interesting for you,' Pannwitz said mockingly. 'I would have thought you had enough boats down there on the Lake?'

'No, no, sir, you don't understand,' the Gestapo man at the Friedrichshafen post said hastily. 'It's not an ordinary kind of a boat–'

'Well, what kind of a boat is it, man,' Pannwitz interrupted the man's excited flow of words, 'get on with it, will you. I'm up to my neck in work here.'

Listening at the extension, the Munich Police Lieutenant told himself sagely that Pannwitz was making a rookie's mistake; he was letting a case get on his nerves.

'It's Swiss, sir. Stolen three days ago from a village on the other side.'

'Swiss!' Pannwitz exclaimed. 'Now that's more like it.'

'And there's more, sir. The men who took it are believed to be the men the *BUPO* is looking for in connection with the murder

185

of the policeman Muessli.'

'What?'

'Yes, well, that's what our – er – people in the *BUPO* tell us at least.'

Pannwitz did some quick thinking. For some unknown reason, the four Englishmen who had killed Muessli on the mountain side, had been involved in the Hirsch affair in Geneva. Now the same four men had apparently come across the Lake to Germany. Why would they undertake anything that risky? The answer was clear. It had something to do with the woman he was looking for. What, he didn't know. But this was the first lead he'd had over the last forty-eight hours and he knew he couldn't afford to neglect it. Holding a hand over the phone, he called, 'Get a car – at once!'

'Where are you intending to go, Colleague Pannwitz?' the Police Lieutenant asked. 'I need the destination for the document.'

'Friedrichshafen, man. Friedrichshafen!...'

The local Gestapo man was very tall and very thin, with a deathly pale face and a long, red dripping nose. To Pannwitz he looked as if he were suffering from acute constipation. He also moved as if Pannwitz's unkind diagnosis might be correct. 'Well, there's the boat, *Herr Oberkommissar*,' he announced importantly, and tugged at the end of his long nose.

'How perceptive you are,' Pannwitz said sardonically, and stepped into the Swiss boat. Curiously, he turned over the four domed masks. 'What are they for?' he asked.

The thin official explained.

'*So, so,*' Pannwitz mused, noting the long scratches on the one which was supposed to represent Punch. Obviously the Tommy with the hook had worn that one. 'And when this old man who found the boat took you to the spot where it had been beached, you discovered nothing?'

'Yes and no,' the other man said, another dewdrop forming at the end of his pointed nose.

'What do you mean?'

'At the spot where the boat was – nothing. But we did search the surrounding empty houses. One of them had been occupied recently. We found food remains – and this.' Like a amateur magician who hoped finally to make one of his tricks work, he opened his hand. On the dirty palm, there was a brass lipstick container.

Pannwitz's heart missed a beat. It *must* belong to her! Ever since the Führer had decreed that '*eine deutsche Frau raucht und schminkt sich nicht,* lipstick had become a rare commodity in Germany, especially since the war industry needed all the fats it could lay its hands on.

Just in time he prevented himself from

snatching it out of the other man's hand. 'Let me see that, please,' he said, forcing himself to appear casual.

Swiftly he turned the little brass tube round. There it was. *Made in Switzerland.* It had been the girl's all right. Now the five of them were on the run *inside* Germany.

'All right, get to the nearest official phone at once.'

'Sir!' the tall man stamped to attention, scattering dewdrops in all directions.

'I want you to contact Frontier Police Headquarters-South. Request that all borders be sealed immediately to Switzerland. Then get on to the local police all along the Lake. Every boat must be placed under guard. Alert the Water Police too.'

'Do you think they'll attempt to cross the Lake?'

Pannwitz shook his head. 'Not them. They'll run for it, and by God, this time we'll be waiting for them!' His pale blue eyes blazed with energy and a sense of triumph; yet all the same he could not quite suppress the little voice inside his head which was asking annoyingly, *'But where?'*

It was the same question that had overwhelmed Cain, at that terrible moment when they had discovered the boat was gone. It wouldn't be long before the German police came looking for them. For the next two hours they had run, swinging round Friedrichshafen to go deeper into the wooded hills that lay beyond the town, forcing themselves to keep up with the killing pace that Cain set, knowing that they must put as much distance as possible between themselves and their hiding place. Now, as they plodded at a slower pace through the snow-heavy trees, by a small track which ran parallel to the secondary road leading to Ravensburg, Cain had begun to form a rudimentary plan. It was time to stop and brief them. They all needed a rest, especially the girl, he told himself.

Thus they crouched now, in the shelter of a clump of thick fir trees, their sweat-lathered faces a gleaming pale-silver in the light of the moon, and waited expectantly for his instructions.

Cain hesitated. He knew they weren't going to like what he had to say and that there would be protests; but he knew, too, that he must keep a firm grip on them, particularly at this moment when their hopes had been dashed and they were frightened. 'Now, I'm assuming,' he began carefully, 'that by now they've found the boat. I could kick myself for not having camouflaged it better. But that's water under the bridge. Anyway, we can safely presume that they are looking for us.'

The girl shivered and Abel pressed her

hand reassuringly. 'Not you, Miss Hirsch,' Cain said quickly. 'They'll be looking for the four of us. There is nothing to associate you with us. Your mother is still safe.'

'I understand, but I had so hoped it was all over.' There was a hysterical catch in her voice. 'All this running and hiding.' Rosamund Hirsch knew she would begin to cry in a moment, if she didn't so something. Desperately she bit into her bottom lip until she could feel the blood begin to flow. The tears did not come.

Cain waited patiently; then he continued. 'Now the question is, what will they expect us to do? I don't think they will be able to launch a mass search operation for us. This is a big stretch of country and pretty rugged once you get away from the Lake, according to the map. So obviously they will group their forces where they anticipate we will attempt to cross into Switzerland – the Lake itself, naturally.'

'But we'll play it different, sir?' Spiv asked, his cunning mind already running over the possibilities.

'Right. The Lake's out altogether.'

'Where then, skipper?' Abel flashed.

'Schaffhausen.'

'Schaffhausen, sir!' Spiv exclaimed. 'But that's a bloody good fifty miles from here!'

'Watch yer tongue, laddie,' Mac warned.

But Spiv was too angry and excited to

note the warning. 'All of us are buggered as it is, sir. We ain't had any proper grub for nearly three days and in the last couple of hours, you've run the plates of meat off us. Now you expect us to hoof another ruddy fifty miles!'

It was the reaction that Cain had expected and he was prepared for it. 'Hold on, Spiv. I'm not going to take the direct route. I intend using the secondary roads and pushing deeper into the hills, swinging in via Stockach and Singen, then down to Schaffhausen. That should be another fifty on top of the original fifty!' He smiled at them.

'A hundred sodding miles!' Spiv moaned. 'Oh, my poor aching back.'

'We'll never make it, skipper,' Abel protested hotly. 'I mean we're fit, and it'll be hell for us. But what about Miss'

'But we're not going to walk,' Cain interrupted him. 'We're going to ride. We're going to find wheels.'

'Wheels?' Abel asked mystified. 'But where?'

Cain pointed to the little winding gravel road that led up from the plain below. 'There!'

It was now nearly midnight. Twice, lonely cars had gone by, but each time Spiv, one hundred yards further down the road, had whistled the alarm signal. In both cases there were too many people in the vehicles for them to tackle safely. Now they could hear the clash of gears and the straining sound of an engine beginning the long ascent.

Cain forgot the cold and his tiredness. He was keyed up too much. They had to find their wheels soon and be on their way. They had to be in the neighbourhood of Singen and under cover by first light. Time was running out for them fast.

Now he could hear the car gathering speed as it came to the straight stretch. Soon the driver would be passing Spiv's hiding place. Cain tensed. In spite of the freezing night, he found himself sweating suddenly. He forced himself to be calm. If Spiv didn't whistle his warning in exactly five seconds, it would be safe to tackle the car. He started to count. *One, two ... five.* Still no warning whistle. They could go ahead with the plan!

'Okay, quick,' he ordered.

They needed no urging. They knew, too, how vital it was for them to be on their way soon. Hastily the three of them and the girl heaved at the heavy log, which they'd balanced against the tall fir nearest the road. 'Now!' Cain commanded.

They let go. The log toppled over and hit the road with a crash, falling exactly into place and blocking the whole road. Cain held his breath. Had the driver heard the noise?

He hadn't. They ducked, as the little Opel Wanderer swept round the sharp bend in second gear, its blacked-out headlights lighting up the road in two narrow slits of blue light.

For what seemed an endless time, the driver did not see the big log barring the way. 'For Chrissake,' Spiv, crouched next to Cain in the ditch whispered, 'the bastard must be as blind as a bloody bat!'

Then the driver saw it. His foot hit the brake. The tyres squealed their protest as the little car swung round violently to the right and skidded to a stop, balancing on the edge of the deep drainage ditch.

'Quick!' Cain snapped.

They rushed forward.

'What's going on?' a shaken, fat-bellied man in the brown uniform of the SA, his chest covered in decorations, called, beginning to open his door. 'I'm County Leader Damm–' But County Leader Damm was not able to finish his introduction. Mac lunged forward. Grabbing him in one of his huge paws, he dragged the little fat man out of his seat and thrust his crimson face close to the German's abruptly, deathly white one. 'Hold yer whish,' he cried in English, 'or I'll have the tongue off ye, my wee mon!'

County Leader Damm might not have understood the words, but he understood the tone well enough. He held his 'whish'.

Thereafter things happened swiftly. The three of them thrust the log to one side while Mac removed the County Leader's belt and braces, leaving him holding up his breeches with trembling hands. Mac and Spiv slid into the back seat. Cain turned to Abel. 'Ask him how far it is to Konstanz?' he snapped.

'Is that wise?'

'Certainly. It would put them off for a couple of hours at least, once he gets back to his own people. Or do you want to deal with him here and now, Abel?' Cain's hand dropped significantly to the pocket containing his pistol.

The County Leader's face blanched. Abel shrugged. 'Okay, have it your own way, Cain.'

He posed Cain's question and the SA man answered in a voice that shook badly. In a minute he would be on his pudgy knees wringing his hands for mercy, Cain thought contemptuously. But he made a face, as if he were considering the information seriously. 'All right, you can go. Hop it!'

'Danke ... danke, mein Herr!' the man quavered, as if he could hardly believe his own luck.

'Bugger off!' Cain aimed an angry kick at the man's fat backside.

Holding up his baggy breeches, the fat man started to trot down the road the way he had come, as if the devil himself were behind him. 'All right,' Cain called, 'you can come out now.'

Swiftly the girl broke from the trees and got into the car next to Abel in the driver's seat. 'Okay,' Cain ordered, 'let's get on with it. Take her off!'

They had their 'wheels'. They were on their way...

TWO

It was nearly dawn now. Behind them Ravensburg lay still sleeping, with only an occasional lazy trickle of dark-brown smoke ascending into the flat white wash of the morning sky. The road ahead, which was already beginning to climb once more into the wooded foothills, was empty, and showed hard, dry and white in the freezing pre-dawn air. In the back of the little car, the initial tension had worn off and Cain and the other two were snoring gently on each other's shoulders. But up front Abel and the girl were wide awake, intent on putting as many kilometres as possible between them and the place where they had hijacked the Opel. Before full daylight, they would be forced to abandon it and go into hiding. Softly the two of them conversed, as if they had been friends for years. Abel was telling her about his days as a young instructor of modern languages in the States, and how at the great rally in New York, he had decided to throw up everything and go to Spain to fight with the Abe Lincoln Battalion in 1937. Suddenly she interrupted him with an alarmed: 'car ahead, coming up to the crossroads!' Abel flashed a swift look ahead. To the right a big black open tourer was speeding for the crossroads in front of them, a silver-metal aerial switching back and forth on its boot. *'Trouble!'* he yelled above the sudden roar of their own motor, as he pressed his foot down hard on the accelerator.

Cain woke immediately. Who would be driving an open tourer in this cold and with a car radio as well? Only police or an official car of some sort. He pulled out his pistol. Next to him Mac and Spiv hastily did the same. 'Knock out the side window, Mac,' he ordered and instantly ripped open the little plastic rear window with his hook. Icy cold air streamed in. But they did not feel it. They were concentrating on the crossroads and the big black car which was approaching it at tremendous speed. The reason was obvious. It was going to try to cut them off!

Abel drove like a madman, with all the skill of the young American of his time, who had owned his first old jalopy at the age of fourteen. He took the insides of all the bends, more than once bulling the little car through on two wheels, the tyres shrieking their protest. Now the crossroads loomed up ever larger. The other car, too. Cain, poised at the window, could just make out white blobs which were faces, behind the rolled up windows. At that speed, the car's aerial was slashing back and forth through the air like a whip. The car must be doing at least sixty miles an hour. He clenched his hand round the butt of his pistol and yelled above the roar of their engine, 'For Chrissake, Abel, beat him!'

Abel nodded his head swiftly, without taking his eyes off the crossroads. 'Get ready!' he commanded through gritted teeth.

They roared through a clump of firs. For a moment the other car vanished from sight. Then they were through again. Cain could make out the signs – *'Ulm'* to the right; *'Bodensee'* to the left. The black tourer was only a hundred yards away, charging up the road towards them. Cain groaned out loud. Abel wouldn't be able to make it. The other car would cut them off. Instinctively he braced his feet against the floor for the moment when Abel must hit the brakes. He was wrong. Abel jammed the accelerator right down. The Opel shot forward. Cain caught a wild glimpse of the driver of the other car as he hit the brake, fighting the big tourer to a stop, as it shimmied crazily from one side of the road to the other. Then they were racing madly for the next curve, followed by a furious chatter of machine pistol fire. They had been right. It had been the police. A moment later the Opel had vanished round the bend. 'Can I pull me stomach down again now, sir?' Spiv gasped. 'It's sodding well floating somewhere above me head.' The others laughed. But they knew they were not out of trouble yet. Behind them, hidden by the bend, they could hear the clash of gears and whine of rubber, as the driver of the other car righted it and swung up the road after them.

Swiftly Abel changed down to third. Before them lay a long stretch of straight, but steep road. He intended to get as much power as possible from the Opel's little engine. Behind them the Mercedes swung round the bend. The driver saw the long straight stretch. He put his foot down, obviously confident that his three litre motor would enable him to overtake the Opel easily before they hit the next bend. The Mercedes started to eat up the distance between the two cars.

'Bollocks,' Spiv cursed, 'here they come again!' He thrust his little Belgian pistol through the open flap of plastic and prepared to fire.

Behind them the dark swaying figure next to the driver rolled down his window and leaned out dangerously, levelled a machine pistol at them. 'Look out, Abel!' Cain yelled in alarm.

Abel reacted instinctively. Just in time he swung the little car to the right. The three of them at the back were thrown to the floor. Lead hissed through the air. To their right, the rock face splintered and holed. But the burst had missed them completely. 'Listen, Cain,' Abel yelled above the roar of the motors, 'they're going to catch us soon… If I can make the next bend, I'm going to hit the anchors.'

'Yes?'

'That'll give you guys one chance to stop them. Okay?' He pressed down ever harder on the accelerator, willing the little car to make it to the bend first; in the mirror, Cain could see sweat pouring down his forehead with the effort.

'Got you!' Cain bellowed back.

Swiftly the three of them righted themselves and took up their firing positions at the rear window. The big black Mercedes was only thirty odd yards away now. They could see the black leather coats and tall felt hats of its occupants quite clearly. They were Gestapo all right.

The gap between the two cars grew even less. The Mercedes cut down the distance with all the arrogance of its big engine. Next to the driver, the man with the Schmeisser balanced himself for the killing burst. They could see how he bared his teeth in impending triumph. Abel slammed home second gear. They were coming into the bend now. It was going to be a hairpin one. The Mercedes' driver reacted a little too late. He had to tap the brakes to get the first corner. The distance between them dropped away to forty yards, as the Mercedes changed with an angry crash. 'Good work, Abel!' Cain cried in approval.

'Get ready!' Abel yelled back through gritted teeth, his hands gripping the wheel, which trembled violently as they swung into the second part of the bend. To their left there was a wooded face; to their right a sheer drop. If his brakes failed him or weren't true, the Opel would go sailing over the side. But Abel knew there was no other alternative. As the Mercedes came tearing round the second bend, just as they vanished beyond the third, he cried at the top of his voice, '*NOW!*'

Holding the wheel tightly in both hands, bracing himself back hard against the seat, he pressed his foot down madly on the brake. For a moment nothing happened. The Opel went sliding on on the loose gravel of the road. But it was running true, not deviating to the side of the road. And then it had stopped and the Mercedes was roaring round the bend, thirty yards away. The German driver hit the brakes, his face contorted with terror, as he saw the little car blocking the road ahead.

In that same moment, the three of them in the back seat fired. At that range they couldn't miss. The driver's face disappeared in a sudden spider's web of shattered glass. Blinded, the German driver fought the car. Cain could hear the wicked grab of protesting, burning rubber on the loose gravel. Too late! *'There she blows!'* Spiv yelled exuberantly, as the helpless Mercedes rushed by them and shot over the side of the road.

They did not see the rest, but they could smell the sickening stench of burning rubber and hear the long-drawn out crash as the Mercedes hit first one rock outspur then another, trailing behind it the sound of shattering glass and ripping, tearing metal, till finally it hit the bottom and came to rest, leaving behind a loud, echoing silence and the thin persistent wail of the jammed horn.

For a moment not one of them was capable of moving. They were too shocked; it had been such a close thing. But finally Cain forced himself to move. He opened the door and staggered out, followed by the others. The three of them seemed to have aged visibly. Together with Spiv, he walked across the road, burnt black with tyre tracks, while

Abel comforted a quietly sobbing Rosamund Hirsch.

What was left of the car, its nose con-
certinaed, had come to rest a couple of
hundred feet below, a long trail of wreckage
and torn-up earth marking its fatal progress
down the hillside. A dark figure lay sprawled
out near the driver's seat, in an ungainly
posture. There was no movement in the
wreckage. They were all dead, he knew that
instinctively, without having to clamber
down to find out.

'Well that settled their hash for them,' Spiv
commented, his voice not quite steady.

'Ay, and it settled our hash for us, too,'
Mac growled behind them.

'What do you mean, Mac?' Cain spun
round.

The big Scot was pointing at the offside
wheel and Cain could hear the thin hiss of
escaping air. He didn't need to be told what
had happened. With their last shots, the
Gestapo had holed the tyre and they had no
spare; he knew that already. *Damn, damn,
damn!'* he cursed and slapped the side of his
hook against the car's roof angrily. 'What
bloody bad luck!'

'Ay, ye can say that agen,' Mac commented dourly. 'But what are we gonna do
now?'

Cain considered rapidly. The question was
whether the dead Gestapo men had con-

tacted their headquarters and reported that they had spotted the County Leader's missing car? He knew that both German military and police radio communications were years ahead of the British. It was quite possible that they would have such a link-up, which was unknown in England outside of London. If they *had* – and he must assume they had – it wouldn't be long before they were sending out another vehicle to check what had happened to the missing Mercedes. 'All right,' he snapped, fully recovered once again. 'Let's assume that they have reported our last position. Accordingly we've got to get the hell out of here.'

'Very smartish!' Spiv agreed, casting an anxious look at the valley below, as if he could already visualize their pursuers looking for them in force.

'How?' Mac snapped. 'Not in this buggered-up crate? It'll get us down the hill and then,' he shrugged, 'we've got to run for it. Come on, let's get her moving!'

Looking not unlike one of the battered old cars that the popular comedy team Laurel and Hardy liked to use in their movies, the little Opel began to limp and jolt its way down the rest of the hill.

THREE

'Of course it was them!' Pannwitz snapped at the thin Gestapo man with the red, running nose. 'They are real killers I've seen that with my own eyes. They would stop at nothing. How many of the car crew were killed?'

'All four of them and young Fritz Deschener had just got married. He'd got the burgomaster's daughter in the pudding club–'

'Shut up!' Pannwitz barked. 'I can't hear myself think with you drivelling on like a shitty old washerwoman!'

'Ich bitte um Verzeihung, Herr Oberkommissar,' the thin man quavered and wiped yet another dewdrop off his long nose with the back of his hand.

Pannwitz ignored him. He strode over to the big map of the Lake Constance area on the wall and stared hard at it, as if by the sheer force of his gaze he could extract the information he needed so desperately, from it.

The fat 'golden pheasant's' guess that they were on their way to Konstanz because of the question they had asked him was a lot of rubbish, of course. A deliberate if somewhat

204

elementary attempt to throw them off. He, Pannwitz, didn't buy pathetic feints like that. But where in three devils' names were they going?

His eyes traced the route they had taken up to their last sighting on the other side of Ravensburg. Why, he told himself, they were going away from the frontier instead of attempting to get down to the Lake. Why? Didn't they realize that with every hour longer they stayed in the Reich, their chances of pulling it off grew progressively worse?

He frowned angrily at the big map. In the old days, it would have been no problem. He would have requested the *Wehrmacht* to throw a huge search force into the area; then they would soon have rooted them out. But this was 1943, the German Army was bleeding to death in Russia, and men were in short supply. Only a month ago, *Reichsfuhrer SS* Himmler, his senior boss, had ordered the formation of a whole division of 17 year old youths from the Hitler Youth, *die Hitlerjugend,* because the manpower barrel was about scraped clean.

Now with the limited police and Gestapo forces at his disposal, attempting to comb the thick wooded hills around the Lake – he didn't have the men for that. He would have to outthink them, wait for them to come back to the Lake again and then grab them.

Konstanz was out. There would be water to cross and he was certain that he had every boat on the German side of the Lake safely locked up. Even if they did manage to steal one, the fast-moving craft of the *Wasserschutzpolizei* would pick them up long before they could ever make it to the Swiss side.

There was, of course, the land routes, the direct link between the Reich and Switzerland. He bent closer to the map. There was Lindau naturally – and Schaffhausen. He sucked his teeth for a moment. There was a devil of a long frontier section to be covered there in both places. He knew the types of defences used: half-wild dogs, long stretches of wire, pinned firmly to the ground with alarm bells on the top; frequent patrols. All the same, escaping Allied POWs had got through them often enough in these last few years, not to mention a sizeable number of treacherous deserters from the *Wehrmacht* who could not face the prospect of Russia. It could be done and he could no longer afford to make any more mistakes. That very morning, Gestapo Mueller, calling from Berlin, had made the not very subtle threat that there was a vacant post at the Gestapo Post at Kiev – 'with no promotion prospects'. He had to find the British bastards soon or face the music.

Then he had it. His face lit up and his big

hand crashed down against his raised knee. 'Of course,' he exclaimed, 'heaven, arse and twine, why didn't I think of it before!'

The thin official stared at him, as if he had suddenly gone off his head. 'Is there anything up ... er ... *Herr Oberkommissar?*' he asked morosely.

'Yes, everything's up!' Pannwitz cried, his fat pink face gleaming happily. 'Have you got a civvie phone here?'

'No, but the police HQ next door has.'

'*Ausgezeichnet!*' Pannwitz chortled. 'Now, get yourself over there and book me a call to Switzerland. At once.'

'Switzerland?'

'Yes, *SWIT ... ZER ... LAND!*' Pannwitz spelled it out for him. 'Now give your arse some air – and move it!'

The skinny official moved it.

Pannwitz beamed at himself in the mirror. This time nothing would go wrong. He'd pull them in, the lot of them and there would be no more talk of shitty Kiev with its stinking promotion prospects, by *Christ there wouldn't!*

FOUR

All that afternoon they had been marching through the deep forests, heading south-west towards the Swiss frontier.

There was no wind. All the same it was bitterly cold in the snow-heavy pines; and the going was bad. But Cain in the lead allowed no respite. He knew that they had to be in position at the frontier by nightfall. It was only under the cover of the darkness that they could chance crossing.

Now their chatter had died away altogether. There was no sound save the crunch of their shoes over the frozen snow and their harsh breathing, as they concentrated all their energies on marching forward.

About 4.00 pm it started to snow; a solid streaming wall of white. Cain was glad of the extra cover. But he knew too the extra effort of marching through the snow was taking the heart out of them, especially the girl. They stumbled on.

The hour that followed was a nightmare of back-breaking exhaustion. Gasping, lungs labouring like very old men, they stumbled, staggered to their feet again, and forced their pain-wracked bodies to continue, peering exhausted through the swirling white mass at the feet of the man in front, keeping going by sheer willpower.

The girl, soaked to the skin, her skirt hanging bedraggled, stockings torn and laddered, began to hang further and further behind. Abel dropped back to support her. But her steps faltered ever more. The pace of the whole group slackened. Angrily Cain looked at his watch. In an hour's time it would be dark. 'Try to keep up – for God's sake,' he called back and plunged on ruthlessly.

Abel, wheezing like a far gone asthmatic himself, tried to support the girl more. But by now she was a dead weight on his shoulder, dragging her frozen, snow-heavy feet behind her, like ton weights. Finally, before he could catch her, she pulled herself from his clutch and sank to the snow. 'I can't … can't go on,' she gasped and let her head sink to her breast. 'I'm done.'

'Rosamund, *please!*' Abel cried desperately and knelt down by her side, the snow streaming down on their heads, *'please!'* Her only response was to shake her head with infinite weariness.

'Stop!' Cain commanded and held up his hand.

Mac and Spiv flopped down in the snow on their faces, gratefully, their shoulders heaving with the effort of drawing breath.

Cain stamped through the snow to where Abel was trying to support the girl against a tree. 'What's the matter with that damned woman?' he demanded.

Abel looked up at him, his eyes full of hatred. 'Can't you see? She's beat – plain beat!'

Cain looked down at him coldly. 'Then get her to her feet, since you've chosen to play Fairy Godmother at the moment.'

'You bastard, Cain!' Abel hissed. 'Can't you ever let up? Haven't I just said she's all in?'

'Then we must leave her here,' Cain answered though he knew they couldn't afford to leave the girl behind; she was too dangerous. But Abel must be forced into a reaction which would get her moving again.

'Jesus, Cain, even you couldn't be that heartless!'

'I've to think of the whole team,' Cain replied, his face hard and set. 'Get her on her feet. I don't care how, but get her walking again!'

Abel swallowed hard. Cain's face remained as rigid as granite and Abel knew there was no moving him. He turned to the girl and raised her head gently. She looked at him, her eyes lifeless, the snow melting and sliding down her frozen cheeks like white tears. 'Rosamund, you've got to get up and move,' he whispered. 'It's not far now. Honest!'

She shook her head slowly. 'I can't … can't.' Her head fell on her chest again.

'Hit her!' Cain commanded harshly. 'It's the only way. You have to be cruel to be kind.'

'No.'

'Then I will.' Cain raised his hand.

Abel caught it before he could bring it down across the girl's face. 'By God, Cain,' he hissed vehemently, 'I'll kill you, if you dare lay a finger on her. I swear I will.'

Cain remained unmoved. Coldly he removed Abel's hand from his arm. 'I'll give you thirty seconds. Then we're leaving.' Abel opened his mouth as if in protest, then closed it quickly. He raised his hand and grasped the girl's bedraggled hair. 'Rosamund,' he cried desperately, tugging up her face, 'you must get to your feet. *You must!*' She didn't react. Suddenly he lashed his other hand across her face. 'Get up, you bitch!' he yelled.

Her eyes flashed open. 'What–'

He hit her again. Her cheeks flushed a bright red. 'Why are you doing this?' she gasped, staring at the American's contorted face, his eyes full of tears.

'To move you.'

'But I can't!'

'*You can!*' He hit her again – hard, giving vent to his rage at her, Cain, the world, for making him have to do this.

'You swine,' she cried. 'Oh, can't you leave me alone.'

'Get up,' he commanded gruffly. 'You're all right. You can walk.' He grabbed hold of her unceremoniously and dragged her to her feet. She swayed dangerously, but didn't fall again. 'Now,' Abel snapped, 'you're going to walk in front of me – and you're not going to stop until I order you to. Move!'

Hesitantly the girl began to walk forward. Mac and Spiv got to their feet and did the same, heads bent against the streaming, merciless white snow.

'Good work, Abel.' Cain gave him a wintry smile.

'Bastard,' was Abel's sole comment.

They reached Stockach, about forty kilometres from Schaffhausen, just after dark. In a daze they staggered through the collection of dirty-white cottages, their roofs heavy with snow, which made up the village. Cain knew now that they would never make the frontier before daylight came. They would have to find some place to hide for the night and try again on the following night. But first they must get through the village. Perhaps on the other side they might be able to find a shed or outhouse where they could lie up for the night. Thereafter there was a clear run through the forest, according to the map, until they reached the last frontier town on the German side, Singen.

Doggedly he plodded on in the lead through the deserted streets. Everywhere the blackout shutters were down turning the place into a dead village. Cain was confident that he could get the group through without difficulty, although they presented a strange appearance in their exhausted, soaked state. But that was not to be.

They were just passing the blacked out little station, the last building before they reached the hills which surrounded Stockach, when a thin blue light snapped on in front of them and a harsh voice demanded, *'Wir sind Sie?'*

Cain started as a bulky, tall figure detached itself from the shadow cast by the station. There was no mistaking the object in his hand – a pistol.

'Travellers,' Abel stammered unconvincingly. 'We're on our way to Singen.'

The blue beam swept to his face. 'At this time of the night and in this weather?' the harsh voice said scornfully. 'Why didn't you take the train, eh?'

Cain prepared to move. But the unknown man was quicker. 'I think you'd all better put your hands up – *now!'* Cain heard the slight click as the man pushed off the safety catch. Wearily he raised his hands. They'd had it!

A minute later they were crowding into the little stationmaster's office, heated by a pot-bellied stove in the corner, being stared at by an awed elderly railway official and his skinny mate, as if they had just landed from the moon. But their captor in the blue uniform of the Railway Police was not awed. He was a big, middle-aged man with the bull-neck, waxed Prussian moustache and medals of a World War One N.C.O. and he was unpleasantly efficient. Within seconds he had discovered their pistols and lack of papers, and had realized that he had caught 'some big fish', as he explained to the wide-eyed civilians in an aside.

Vainly Abel tried to convince him that they were escaped British POWs. But the scornful look on the Railway Policeman's face showed he didn't believe them. 'What, escaped POWs – with a German woman-friend.' With his free hand he tapped his forefinger to his temple, German fashion. 'Do you think I've not got all my cups in my cupboard!'

'What are you going to do with them, Fritz?' the wide-eyed elderly railway official asked. 'You know the phone's down to Konstanz!'

Cain's heart missed a beat. Did that mean the fat cop couldn't contact the real police and that they had a chance before they disappeared behind bars in a police cell? Fritz guffawed. 'What am I supposed to want the Konstanz police for?' he growled. 'A lot of asparagus Tarzans, they are!' He puffed out his big chest. 'I'll take care of this little lot myself tonight, and have 'em out on the first train to Konstanz myself, tomorrow morning. Why should those fat-arsed pen-pushers in Konstanz get all the credit!'

'But where are you going to put them for the night, Fritz?' the civilian protested. 'We ain't got any cells here.'

Cain repressed a sigh of relief just in time.

'I know, I know. But we've got a lot of rope, ain't we, and a nice well-built brick equipment shed, haven't we? You,' he nodded at the skinny mate, 'double off and get me some rope.'

Five minutes later the two civilians had trussed up the four Ultra men, tying their wrists to their ankles under the policeman's skilled direction, while he kept his pistol levelled at the Englishmen. They then deposited them in the tool shed, which was attached to the office by a little passage.

'What about the woman?' The skinny one asked when they returned to the room. 'Her, too?'

Fritz grinned and licked his thick red lips in pleasurable anticipation, his little pig's eyes fixed on Rosamund Hirsch's breasts. 'Of course, but I'll reserve that little pleasure

215

for myself.' He stuck his pistol in its holster and advanced on her. 'What do they say? – *mitgegangen, mitgefangen, mitgehangen…*'

FIVE

Rosamund Hirsch swung her bound feet against the wooden door angrily.

'What's going on in there?' the Railway Policeman's muffled voice called. 'Can't I get a bit of shut-eye, eh?'

The girl didn't answer. While the others watched her with anxious eyes, she kicked the door once again.

'In God's name, what are you lot doing in there – dancing the damned polka?'

There was a low rumble of tired laughter at the policeman's sally and one of the civilians commented that 'Fritz' was a 'real old comedian'.

'I must go to the lavatory,' the girl called urgently, *'please!'* She kept her gaze firmly fixed on the floor, her cheeks suddenly burning hotly. Abel flashed her a look of sympathy, but Cain kept his eyes fixed firmly on the locked door. Would the cop fall for it?

'All right … all right,' the Railway Policeman answered. There was a scrape of a wooden chair being thrust back lazily. 'Hold yer water, Fraulein.'

There was another burst of laughter from the others and a moment later the door was flung open. The Railway Policeman stood there, one hand on his pistol, the other tugging at his half-open tunic. He looked down at the girl, his eyes a mixture of caution and contempt. 'Well?'

She looked up at him, her cheeks a fiery red, playing the role of her life. 'Must I beg you,' she said urgently. 'I can't stand much more! I have to go – *now.*' The man sighed. 'Oh, all right. But no funny business, eh?' He bent down and began to loosen the rope around her ankles so that she could at least hobble. 'You lot, don't sit there like dum-dums. Keep them covered with the pistols,' he raised his voice and shouted at the two civilians.

The two men pulled out the pistols they had taken from the Ultra team and levelled them with trembling hands, almost as if they expected the helplessly trussed up captives to rush them at any moment.

The Railway Policeman completed his work and hauled the girl to her feet. 'All right, come on.'

Awkwardly she hobbled behind him to the door with the double 'O' on it, indicating that it was the toilet. He flung it open.

'There!' he announced.

She took in the dirty sink and lidless lavatory pan. Obviously the place was used by Railwaymen on night shift. She flashed him a pleading look. 'In heaven's name, can't I have the door closed?'

The policeman considered a moment, tugging at his heavy chin ponderously, as if he were making a decision of considerable importance. 'All right,' he said finally. 'There's no getting out of there. I'll close it.'

Contemptuously he rammed his heavy boot against the door. The door slammed closed behind her. 'And don't take too damned long either,' he yelled.

'Thank you. I won't,' she cried, her eyes already beginning to search the little room swiftly.

A staple of cut-up newspaper. *Der Volkische Beobachter*, ending in its rightful place, she couldn't help thinking. She turned round and fumbled with the nail that held the leaves to the wall. It was too tightly embedded for her to get it out. Hastily she turned her attention to the sink. A newspaper photo of a group of Hitler Maidens, suitably scantily clad, at some game or other, was fixed in the corner of the fly-blown mirror above it. Her gaze swept along the ledge above it. There was no forgotten razor blade there. She dropped her eyes to the sink itself, its bowl rimmed with the grey grease of generations of railwaymen. A bit of iron hard wartime ersatz soap and a mug, its inside deep-brown from coffee.

'How much longer?' The Railway Policeman demanded from outside. 'I want to get my head down again.'

'Be straight out,' she called desperately.

As best she could, she grasped the mug in one bound hand, and hopped over to the lavatory. With her free hand she pulled the rusty chain. There was a great noisy rush of water, and simultaneously, she let the mug drop on the dirty stone floor. It shattered immediately. Her heart racing excitedly, she bent down and found what she wanted, an instant before the Railway Policeman flung open the door, crying, 'What's this? Do you need any help pulling up your knickers?' He stopped short, the smile vanishing from his face to be replaced by a look of suspicion. 'Hey what's going on here?' he demanded gruffly.

'I stumbled against the sink,' she answered. 'I'm very sorry, I–'

'Oh, knock it off,' he interrupted her. 'But there'll be no more lav for you, my good Miss. You can pee yer pants for all I care next time.'

Outside the two civilians laughed coarsely. But now she didn't care; she had what Cain wanted.

'Aufstehen!'
The Railway Policeman rammed his big

foot against the door, and roared his command once again. 'Time to raise your little curly heads.'

'Go and crap in yer cap!' Spiv called coarsely and yawned. 'Waking people in the middle of the night like this!'

'Four o'clock,' the Railway Policeman yelled. 'Express to Konstanz comes through in thirty minutes and you lot are going to be on. All right, I'm opening the door now. And no monkey business. Or yer won't live to be on the train.'

Cain yawned. Next to him Abel, his eyes alert and anxious, did the same. In the corner, Mac was still apparently fast asleep, his big chest rising and falling regularly, as if he were sleeping on a soft mattress, instead of a hard concrete floor.

The door was flung open. Yellow light from the other room streamed in. The Railway Policeman stood there, framed by it, his fat face a gleaming, freshly-shaven, lobster-pink, his 'Kaiser Bill' moustache bristling and black with new wax. In his hand he held his pistol. Behind him the two armed railwaymen waited attentively for his next order. He frowned angrily at the still sleeping Mac. 'What's up with that swine?' he demanded. 'He must be deaf!'

He bent down, his belly full of fresh coffee, laced with rum, his gleaming face bright and confident that he had the situation well in hand. Already he was beginning to picture the surprised looks on the faces of those fat-arsed clerks in Konstanz when he brought in his prisoners. 'Hey, you, deaf-lugs! Wake–'

He never finished the command. Mac's hands shot up from behind his back and wrapped themselves around the fat cop's throat. *'Aach!'* the breath died in the depth of his lungs, as Mac exerted full pressure. He squeezed and squeezed with the terrible strength of desperation.

'Get off, or I'll fire!' the little runt of a civilian called, his whole body trembling violently with shock. He aimed his pistol. The gleaming hook hissed from Cain's good hand. (He had removed it an hour before, once Abel had finally managed to saw through the rope with the sharp-edged piece of pot.) The runt screamed hideously. He staggered back against the stove, the terrible hook protruding from the centre of his forehead. At once the rest of them flung themselves on the remaining man, while on the floor, Mac was no longer a man, but a wild, blood-crazed animal. His teeth gritted, his eyes bursting out of their sockets, his head flung back in order to exert full pressure, he thrust his big cruel fingers deeper and deeper into the Railway Policeman's neck...

They had just finished piling the last of the coke over the bodies of the three dead Germans, when the two red lights and the trembling of the track at their backs, indicated the approach of the express to Konstanz. *'Down!'* Cain yelled urgently.

They ducked behind the great heap of coke, their ears suddenly full of the train's roar. Cain's hand flashed down to his pistol. Had the dead policeman somehow managed to telephone in the village for the express to stop? The roar grew louder and louder, as the dark monster hurtled ever closer to the little station. At Cain's side, Spiv clicked off his safety-catch. All of them knew now what would be in store for them if they were found next to the bodies of the murdered men; the mob would probably lynch them there and then. This had happened to more than one RAF bomber crew shot down over some ruined German city. All of them were prepared to fight to the death!

But the express showed no signs of slowing down. It flashed by them in a flurry of fiery-red sparks and a clatter of steel wheels, sending the loose gravel flying on both sides. A moment later it was two glowing rear-lights, fast disappearing into the pre-dawn gloom.

Abel breathed out hard and thrust his pistol back into his pocket. 'Gee,' he said, 'that was a close one.'

'Close one!' Spiv commented. 'I need a pair of new knickers – that I do.'

'Come on,' Cain snapped, but his voice could not quite disguise his sense of relief. 'Let's get back there and see what Miss Hirsch has found for us to eat. Time's getting on.'

Hastily they crunched back to the little station across the way.

While the girl stood guard at the door, they ate the dark sandwiches – ersatz cheese paste on rough black bread – and listened to Cain's orders. 'According to the timetable outside,' he lectured them, 'the first train to stop here arrives at zero six thirty. So once we've finished this, we've got about ninety minutes to get a good start.' He shrugged hastily. 'Maybe two hours. I guess the local peasants'll take a while before they cotton that all isn't well with the local branch of the *Deutsche Reichsbahn*.'

'And then, sir?' Spiv asked, his mouth full, reaching out for the blackened coffee can, bubbling on the stove.

'We've got to find some place to lie up for the day. The weather's bloody cold, I know, but it's on our side. It'll make it impossible, I should think, for them to use dogs to trace us–'

'What?' Spiv put down the coffee pot hastily. *'Dogs?'*

'Right. Once the authorities find out what has gone on here, you can bet your life, they'll order an all-our search for us. And it won't take them too long to guess where we're heading for, will it?'

Mac nodded his head. 'Ay that it won't. Ay, they Jerries are canny enough for that, in spite of yon squareheads they all have. They'll know weel who we are and where we're going...'

Just how right Mac was, he didn't realize till half an hour later. All of them flopped down hastily into the snow-filled ditch on the other side of Stockach. They were just in time. A moment later a fast-moving black Mercedes swung into view, eating up the kilometres on the road to Switzerland. Their faces buried deep in the snow, their hearts racing crazily, they did not see the face of the man sitting in the back. It was that of *Oberkommissar Heinz Pannwitz!*

SIX

They awoke at five in the afternoon, stiff and trembling with cold. Through the hut's little window, Cain could see that there had been a fresh fall of snow. Good, he told himself, that will make it even more difficult for the dogs. Yawning and trembling at the same time, he pushed back the sack with which he had covered himself and stepping carefully over the others, he crossed to the window.

The trees which were grouped around the lonely hut, were heavy with new snow and beyond, the fields sparkled with it under a suddenly harshly blue sky in which he could already see the pale silver disc of the moon.

'I'll just have a couple of soft-boiled eggs and a pot of tea, James,' Spiv called from the floor. 'But you might bring the paper.'

Cain muttered a mild obscenity and said: 'And you might get your lazy arse out of that pit. It'll be dark enough for us to move off in about thirty minutes. Now look a bit sharpish the lot of you!' They needed no urging. The hut was icy cold. Besides they were refreshed by the afternoon's sleep. With renewed energy, they prepared themselves for the last stage of their march to the border.

Under Spiv's direction, a bundle of yellowing newspapers they had found previously in the corner of the hut, was taken apart and the stiff, smelly sheets tucked under their jackets. 'It'll keep yer warm all right. I know you toffs didn't have to worry about that kind of stuff before the war, but us workers had to keep warm any way we could.'

'*Workers!*' Mac snorted indignantly. 'The only work you ever did was dipping yer long fingers in somebody's till.' All the same he carried out Spiv's instructions faithfully; he knew it was going to be a devilishly cold night. They would need all the warmth they could get.

When they had broken into the hut earlier that day, they had searched for clothes for the girl, but found nothing but a pair of moth-eaten overalls. Now she drew them on and flung a sack over her shoulders to complete the impression. Abel laughed. 'You certainly look as if you've just come off the farm now, Rosamund,' he joked.

She wrinkled up her nose. 'I think I *smell* like it too.'

Finally Spiv distributed the tools he had found in the shed at the back of the hut, remarking that 'in the Kate Karney, the best way to avoid a fatigue, is allus to look as if you're doing something.' He swung the light spade he had claimed for himself over his shoulder. 'All right, don't I look just like an honest Jerry farmer returning home from his honest labours, ready for a bit of grub – and perhaps a little bit of the other with the missus later on?' He beamed at them broadly.

In spite of his inner tension at this the final and most crucial stage of their march to the frontier, Cain could not restrain his laughter.

But Mac, as usual, was not impressed. He wrapped his big ham of a hand around the pick Spiv had given him and said thickly, 'Remember there's ladies present – so watch that evil tongue of yourn, laddie.'

But at that moment Spiv was irrepressible. 'Yes, Daddy,' he answered in a little boy's voice. Laughing at the look of crimson fury on Mac's face, he headed for the door.

By eight o'clock that night they had reached the outskirts of Singen, the last German town before the Swiss border. From his original briefing in England, when Cain had checked up – very fortunately as he realized now – what the state of the Swiss-German frontier was, he recalled that to the west and south of the town, there were thick and he hoped, lonely woods. Through these woods, the second class road and railway line ran directly to Schaffhausen. Indeed, according to the map produced by the MI9 experts, the road formed the Swiss-German frontier in some places.

Cain now ordered the team off the road to Singen, taking a little side road, which he hoped would join the second class frontier one running to Schaffhausen. They obeyed with alacrity. It was exceedingly cold and none of them wanted to stand around discussing the correct course of action. They pushed ahead. Time passed. There was no sound save the crunch of their shoes across the frozen snow and the harsh gasp of each inhaled breath, as they felt the icy air stab painfully into their lungs. To their right, they could see the faint pink glow of Singen's factories above the spiked top of the firs. The place was obviously some sort of industrial town, but the road they were taking was completely empty. Cain, in the lead, began to feel that they would pull it off without trouble. As soon as they were on the Swiss side of the frontier, he would contact Dansey's man at the Embassy in Berne and have him arrange for false documents for them, until it was time for the 131st Squadron's Lysander to pick them up in some secluded spot in the French Jura. He quickened his pace. They couldn't be more than an hour from the frontier now and he was in a hurry to get them across.

They had just linked up with the frontier road when a harsh youthful voice ordered *'Halt!'*

They swung round, as if stung. A thin light snapped on and they could make out three youthful shapes standing in the cover of the snow-heavy pines, clad in the black peaked caps and jackets of the Hitler Youth. 'What are you doing out here at this time of the night?' one of them demanded haughtily, stepping out of the trees, one hand resting on his Hitler Youth dagger.

Under other circumstances, Cain might

have laughed at the boy's nerve – he didn't look a day over fifteen, reached up to Cain's chest, and was confronted by four desperate armed men. But not at this moment. There might be others of them in the woods around and one cry might suffice to alarm the whole neighbourhood.

'We've been working in the forest, son,' Abel said casually.

'In the forest – at this time of the night? You don't come from here either.' The boy cast Abel a keen-eyed look. 'And don't call me son – I'm a Youth Leader.'

'Sorry, Youth Leader,' Abel raised his voice to drown Mac's growl behind him. 'No, we're from the Ruhr. We have been conscripted to help get out timber for pit props. You know how urgently they need them up there?' The boy nodded sagely, as if it were obvious he knew.

'And where do you live?' he asked.

Cain tightened his grip on the axe he carried over his shoulder. But Abel did not hesitate. 'Singen.'

'Yes,' the girl added, her voice deep and masculine. 'Just off the Adolf Hitler Square.' She flung a hurried prayer to heaven in the hope that Singen, like every other German city since the National Socialist takeover in 1933, had renamed one of its streets or squares after the Führer.

'You mean Adolf Hitler *Street*,' the boy said.

'Yes, pardon me.'

The boy ignored the apology. 'All right. Be off with you. Soon it will be curfew and you'll be in trouble if you're caught out without special papers. *Heil Hitler!*' He snapped to attention and flung out his hand, as if he were being presented to the Führer himself at the Nuremberg Party Rally.

'*Heil Hitler!*' they replied through gritted teeth. Abel could feel almost physically the hatred streaming out from a crimson-faced Mac. Cautiously he reached out his heel and pressed it down hard on Mac's toes. Then they were walking quickly down the road towards Singen.

'Whew!' Abel breathed out hard, when the little Hitler Youth patrol had vanished into the darkness behind them. 'That really gave me a scare.'

'Poor little silly buggers,' Spiv commented. 'They ought to be at home with their muvvers around a warm fire instead of being out on a sodding night like this playing soldiers.'

'I would have killed them,' Cain said almost as if he were speaking to himself. 'With the shovel.'

Behind him Abel shuddered and pressed the girl's arm protectively.

They plodded on.

They swung round Singen without incident. The blackout and the coldness of the night provided effective cover; the suburban streets were empty. Skirting the great slag heaps outside the little town, they entered the woods once again and set off southwards for the frontier.

An hour later they emerged from the last of the trees, and saw before them the frontier road, and beyond it a cluster of yellow lights in the distance. 'The Swiss frontier,' Cain whispered and dropped to one knee. The others followed his example and began to search the far side of the little road for obstacles.

'There seems to be some sort of sentry post up to the right, sir,' Spiv announced, after a few moments.

'Where?' Cain demanded.

'There! Looks like somebody's smoking a fag.'

Cain strained his eyes and caught the faint glow of a cigarette end. 'Yes, I can see it now, Spiv. And it's on the Jerry side.' He did a quick calculation and asked, 'How far do you reckon that chap's away from us, Spiv?'

The little cockney shrugged slightly. 'Perhaps fifty yards, sir. Not more.'

'Yes, that's what I thought, too.'

'I don't get it skipper,' Abel said.

'Well, let's assume that they have a sentry post every hundred yards or so on this stretch of road, where it forms the frontier – and surely they couldn't afford the men to have the posts closer than that – then we must be right in the middle of two posts.'

Abel and the rest nodded their understanding.

'So if we can get across without trouble, we have a fair chance of making it through that wire on the other side successfully.'

'Ay, but ye must reckon with link-up patrols, mon,' Mac objected. 'They're canny enough to run mobile patrols between the posts and if we're caught out there in the open–'

'We'd really be up the creek without a ruddy paddle,' Spiv finished.

'Ay,' Mac said grimly.

Cain considered for a moment. He looked at his watch and said, 'We've got another four hours before dawn, so we've plenty of time to study the set-up. We'll move back into the bushes and have a look-see. Once we've worked out their routine, we can decide when to go across.'

Midnight passed. An ancient truck rattled past once, but it seemed to have nothing to do with the frontier posts. The waiting began to strain their nerves almost unbearably. The frontier and freedom were only a matter of yards away – within grasping distance – yet they dared not cross. Now they had the exact position of both posts. Cain's guess had been right. They were exactly in the middle between the two of them. But what was the link between the two groups of sentries? *What?* At one o'clock they found out. There was a sudden challenge from the post to their right and the bark of an NCO turning out the guard.

'The OD,' Abel whispered urgently.

'Of course,' Cain said, the orderly officer doing his rounds. 'Assuming they change the sentries every two hours – two hours on and four off, as we do – he'd be trying to catch the current sentry having a little doze, halfway through his spell of duty.'

'Typical officer's cunning,' Spiv commented scornfully. 'And they call them officers *and gentlemen!*'

But apparently the duty officer had found nothing to complain about, for a few moments later they heard the NCO in charge of the post, bark another order, followed a second later by a faint *'Gute Nacht, Herr Leutnant.'*

'Look out,' Cain hissed urgently. 'He's coming this way.' He caught a glimpse of a shaded blue torch and the next instant he'd buried his face in the snow. The officer was coming down the road towards them, flashing his torch from side to side slowly. He was the link-up between the two posts!

Cain listened to the crisp steps getting ever closer, like a wild beast ready to spring on its prey. He was racked by a terrible inner conflict. In a moment he might have to make an irrevocable decision. If the officer spotted them, they would have to run for it. There was no going back now. In spite of the icy air, he felt himself begin to sweat.

Now the officer had almost reached their hiding place. Suddenly he stopped. Cain froze. Had he seen them? The thin blue light swept the road just in front of them. Cain could just see it. Then the footsteps commenced again. They were safe. For a few moments Cain simply could not speak. Finally, however, he managed to pull himself together. 'All right,' he whispered, 'he's gone.'

'I thought our number was up then,' Spiv said.

'You're not the only one!' Cain straightened up. 'Come on. We're not going to go through that again. Let's go. But keep down.'

Swiftly, followed by the rest, he rushed across the road at the double and flung himself full length in the snow at the other side. No one had seen them. There was no sound save the faint bark of an order at the other post. Obviously the NCO in charge there was turning out the guard for the orderly officer. He began to crawl forward. He made little sound in the snow, but to *his* ears, it sounded so loud that no sentry could possibly miss it. But as he finally reached the wire and started to inspect it, he realized that they had reached the last obstacle without being spotted.

'It looks a tough baby,' Abel whispered in his ear.

Cain nodded grimly. It did. It was nearly four yards high and consisted of tight, thick wire V's, supported at yard intervals by stout iron poles. Worst of all, small bells were hung along the whole length of the fence's top. One touch on the wire and the whole lot would start off like a clarion.

'What do you think, sir?' Spiv asked, his voice not quite steady.

'Well, we can't go over the top for a start,' Cain answered.

'Ay,' Mac agreed, 'Not a bluidy tree with overhanging branches, within yards of the damned thing.'

'Hm,' Cain mused. 'And we have no tools to force open the thing, even if we could silence the bells.'

'What about underneath, skipper?' Abel suggested.

'Yes.' Cain made a decision. 'That's the only way. I'll have a look-see at the base. The rest of you scatter and see if you can pull off a branch or find something so we can start under the damned thing.'

While they slipped away to carry out his orders, Cain, using his hook, and the girl with her hands, began to clear away the hard snow at the base of the fence, revealing that it was pegged to the ground at foot intervals by wooden stakes. The girl put both her hands around one and tugged. It didn't give. 'Must be frozen in,' she hissed.

'Yes. Let me have a go.'

Cain swiftly unscrewed his hook and gripping it firmly in his good hand, swung it at the nearest stake. The sharp hook went deep into it. He grunted and exerted all his strength. The stake came out with a sucking noise, which did not quite drown the faint tinkle of the nearest bell.

The girl caught her breath with fear. Cain froze. He looked up anxiously. But only the one bell had reacted. He breathed out a deep sigh of relief and told himself urgently he'd have to be a damn sight more careful with the next one.

Five minutes later he had freed a three foot stretch of the wire from the pegs, sufficient space for them to begin digging.

They went at it all out, while an anxious-eyed Rosamund Hirsch watched the bells on the top of the fence, ready to stop them instantly at the slightest movement of the bells.

Ten minutes later they had excavated a respectable hole, large enough to allow even the biggest of them – Mac – to crawl under without disturbing the bells.

'All right,' Cain ordered, 'that's enough. Let's try it now before that orderly officer of theirs decides to stroll back this way.' He nodded to the girl. 'Miss Hirsch, we've come

236

a long, long way to fetch you, so I think it's only fair you should go first.'

She bent, and straightening out her body on the snow, thrust her arms cautiously through the hole. 'Am I in the right position?' she whispered.

Spiv opened his mouth to say something, but thought better of it and closed it again.

'Yes,' Cain answered. 'Off you go.'

A moment later she was through soundlessly, brushing away the snow from her knees and elbows.

Spiv followed. The bells remained silent. He straightened up and grinned at them from the other side of the wire. 'Greetings from Switzerland. Wish you were here.'

'Shut up!' Cain hissed. 'You're next, Mac.'

Mac lowered himself a little stiffly and reaching his big hands through began to edge himself forward. But the hole was not as big as Cain had judged it to be. Mac's shoulder struck the wire.

Several things happened at once. The bell directly above the hole tinkled, there was a shout from the direction of the post to their right, and a motorbike engine burst into noisy life.

'*Freeze!*' Cain rapped urgently.

Just in time. A moment later a motorbike flashed by them, heading in the direction of the post to which the officer had gone. Instinctively Cain knew the driver was going to pick up the officer now that his tour of inspection was over.

For five long minutes, which seemed to the rigid Ultra team like five centuries, they waited in utter silence. But their luck seemed to be in that night. Nothing happened. They hadn't been spotted.

Swiftly Cain dug away the earth to Mac's side, while the big Scot, half his body in Switzerland, the other still in Germany, glowered at him. A moment later the hole was big enough to allow him through without further trouble. Cain and Abel followed within seconds. Cain stood there for a moment, shakily. Then a delirious feeling of triumph swamped him. He forgot how cold, how exhausted, how hungry he was. He had done it! He had got them through into freedom and safety!

But he knew no time could be wasted on self-congratulations. They must get on and be out of the border area before dawn. Somewhere further inland, he would find a phone and contact Dansey. The main thing was to get into Schaffhausen and find some cover. After all, they were wanted men in Switzerland too.

He tried to control the trembling of his hand and the hectic thudding of his heart. 'All right,' he ordered hoarsely, 'bury the pistols. We won't need them any more in Switzerland.'

'Isn't that a wee bit dangerous?' Mac protested.

'No, Mac. From now until we can contact our embassy, we're British POWs escaped from Germany, if anybody picks us up.'

'Ay, it would look a bit fishy, if we were found with the pistols,' Mac agreed. He pulled out his and tossed it into the snow. With his big foot he pressed it down deep. The others did the same.

'Feel a bit naked without it,' Spiv said, hesitating momentarily.

'You'll feel something else, if you don't get a move on, Spiv,' Cain snapped. 'Now come on!'

Five minutes later the voice crying out of the darkness, *'Halt – Schweizer Zoll!'* told them that their luck had finally run out.

They had walked straight into a Swiss customs post...

SEVEN

'So, so,' the fat, elderly Customs Sergeant mused, staring at them across the top of his desk, as they sipped the steaming red-hot coffee, which he had pressed on them, 'you are escaped British prisoners-of-war?'

They nodded energetically, encouraged by the coffee and the cigarettes which he and the other half-dozen elderly officials had handed them, once they'd identified themselves inside the snug, warm customs post. Obviously the man was beginning to believe their story.

'You seem to have had a rough time, I can see.'

Again they nodded and assumed a suitably wan look.

'But how does the woman fit into this?' the Customs Sergeant asked, puzzled.

'She helped us with our escape,' Spiv answered, quicker off the mark than the rest. 'She was a Red Cross nurse in the camp.' He bent his gaze modestly. 'She fell in love with me. My charm, my good looks. You understand? One thing led to another and in the end she helped us with the escape.'

The Swiss whistled softly through his teeth and looked significantly at the others. They seemed suitably impressed. 'Oh, you British,' he said fondly, 'cool as a cucumber on the outside, but inside – aha, devils with the women, eh?'

Spiv winked at him slowly.

The Swiss grinned and then was business-like again. 'Well, I shall tell you your rights, according to Swiss Federal Law.' He cleared his throat importantly. 'In accordance with Paragraph 215, Section 3B, escaped prisoners-of-war discovered on Swiss territory will be...'

Happily Cain let the words drone away into the distance. The fat Swiss had bought their story, and he knew what would happen already. They would be handed over to the Swiss Army authorities and interned in one of the big camps in the south, which held mostly French escapees, Jews and a fair number of Anglo-American air crew who had been forced to bail out over Switzerland while on Ops. As he knew from the drill explained to him by MI9, if the Allied prisoner were important enough for the war effort, Swiss doctors bribed by the Embassy would certify that the man concerned was too unfit to fight; thereupon he could be repatriated. Perhaps Dansey's people might be able to pull that one with them. Or maybe they'd find a quicker method of getting the Ultra team back to the UK. But for the time being, it didn't matter how they did it. In the internment camp they would be safe from the Swiss Police. How would they connect the four ragged prisoners-of-war with the rich Englishmen, accused of the *Muessli* murder, who had disappeared from the country, obviously heading for Germany, nearly a week before?

'So you understand your rights, eh?' the Swiss concluded.

'Yes,' they affirmed.

'Good. It is now my duty to ask you whether you have anything to declare. Cigarettes, spirits, perfumes.'

'Oh, my holy Christ, it–' Spiv began. But Cain gave him a quick dig in the ribs to shut him up. They would play this in the pompous, ludicrously unrealistic Swiss way. 'No,' he said, when the Swiss had completed the long list of taxable objects that they might have brought across with them from Germany, 'nothing to declare at all, *mein Herr.*'

'Good, good,' the Swiss beamed at him, then picked up his hat. His men did the same, slinging their rifles, and buttoning up their heavy khaki coats. 'Now we take you to the Main Customs Headquarters at Schaffhausen. Der Herr Oberzollkommissar Deutscherli will arrange for the Army to pick you up.'

'Thank you,' Cain said humbly, as they started to troop out, 'you are very kind.'

'Thick as bloody planks,' Spiv muttered contemptuously, as they clambered into the truck which was to take them and their guards to Schaffhausen. 'Swiss, cor I've shit 'em!'

The sky to the east was a faint dirty white as they arrived in the Swiss border city. It was nearly dawn and the city was slowly coming to life. As the truck started to rumble through

242

the respectable red-brick villas of the suburbs, the weary Ultra men could hear the morning sounds of people waking up: the soft cries of babies, the rattle of a sluggish car engine, the squeak of garage doors being forced open. And everywhere there was the warm, tempting smell of freshly brewed coffee. It was the start of a new day in a country at peace, whose citizens had not heard a shot fired in anger for over two hundred years. Cain grinned lazily. What could one expect from a country like that – but petty, provincial materialism? Still at that particular moment, with all the energy drained out of him by the efforts of the last few days, he did not exactly object to the Swiss concept of the good life.

Five minutes later the truck stopped at the tall modern building, not far from the Schaffhausen Rhine Falls, which housed the Main Customs Offices. They were escorted into the main entrance, the elderly customs men herding them forward with their rifles, a little embarrassed by the looks of the early morning workers, heading for the local machine factories. The official at the desk was obviously expecting them. He nodded to the lift. 'In there,' he said. *'Herr Deut-scherli ist im Bilde.'*

They were escorted to the lift. 'Come and see us after the war, Englishmen, and spend some money here in little Switzerland, eh?'

the elderly customs official shouted, just before the receptionist locked the iron grid behind them and pressed the button.

'We will,' Cain lied, telling himself as the lift began its ascent, that Switzerland would probably be the last country he would visit – if he survived the war.

Oberzollkommissar Deutscherli, a tall, balding man with green eyes, was waiting for them personally as the lift finally stopped on the top floor and they stepped out.

'*Deutscherli,*'he snapped, bowing slightly at the waist, though Cain noticed that he kept his right hand on his pistol holster as he did so, and that the holster was open. 'You are the English prisoners?' he asked unnecessarily in English. His green eyes flicked to the girl.

Cain nodded. 'Yes, we are the prisoners.'

Deutscherli extended his soft hand with the unctuous expertise of a Swiss receptionist, which he'd been before he had decided he could make more money as a customs official. 'Please – enter.'

They entered.

The big sparse room furnished with severe modern furniture, was empty, save for a heavy set man in civilian clothes, who stood with his back towards them. He puffed at his cigarette and stared out at the Falls, through the tall picture window which reached from floor to ceiling. He did not turn round, but continued to smoke, while Deutscherli settled himself behind the big desk. The Swiss official shot back his gleaming white cuffs, linked by overlarge brass cufflinks, and said in a happy voice, 'Come, come, gentlemen, fool me, you cannot.' He laughed, as if he had just heard a good joke, but this green calculating eyes did not light up. 'Prisoners-of-War – you are not.'

Cain's weariness vanished immediately. In spite of the man's pomposity and absurd English, he sensed danger – real danger. 'What do you mean?' he asked, trying to control himself. Beside him, the girl's face had suddenly gone very pale.

The bantering tone had fled from the official's voice when he spoke again; now it was harsh and accusing. 'What do I mean? I am telling you. You are not what you say you are.' He took his green eyes off them and turned to the civilian standing smoking at the big window. *'Aber lieber Heinz, sag' du es den!'*

Slowly, very slowly, as if he had waited a long time for this moment, the civilian turned round to face them.

'Cor ferk a duck,' Spiv gasped. *'Pink-face!'*

The civilian gave him a thin wintry smile. *'Darf ich mich vorstellen,'* he said in a soft voice, *'Oberkommissar Pannwitz, Geheimstaatspolizei!'*

EIGHT

'You see,' Pannwitz said, obviously pleased at the way he had trapped them so unsuspectingly, 'I reasoned that if our security forces didn't succeed in stopping you, our friends in Switzerland would.'

'Friends!' Abel said contemptuously, unable to repress his bitterness, 'you mean traitors, bought for money!'

Deutscherli flushed hotly. 'I object to that,' he snapped, his hand dropping to his holster. 'There are many of us in Switzerland, who feel their first loyalty is to their blood – *German blood* – and not to this absurd, little democracy.'

'Peace, my dear Deutscherli, peace,' Pannwitz interrupted with his raised hand. 'We in Berlin know your sterling qualities. These English and the Jewess do not understand the mystic call of blood. After all, they are just killers.'

'Thank you, Heinz,' Deutscherli answered gravely, as if he had just been awarded that accolade of purity which the Swiss give to those cows which produce the cleanest milk.

Pannwitz turned to the crestfallen pris-

246

oners again. 'Now we know all about you, so I think any further talk on that subject is unnecessary.'

'Yes,' Cain agreed wearily. 'For God's sake get on with it and turn us over to the Swiss Police.'

'Why should we?' Pannwitz said with a little half-smile. 'Do you really want to spend the rest of your lives rotting in some Swiss jail on account of the death of a man who was not really a very worthy individual? The man had the soul of an accountant!'

'What do you mean, Pannwitz?'

'This. I would like to make you a little proposition.' He hesitated a moment, as if uncertain how to formulate the next words. 'You see I would like to take you back with me to Germany. Naturally you have my word of honour as a German officer, (Deutscherli straightened his shoulders automatically at this significant phrase,) 'that your lives will be spared if you answer our questions.'

'Bugger that for a lark,' Spiv muttered under his breath in English. 'We've heard that one before.'

'Why should we?' Cain challenged him. 'One jail is as good as another. And even with the help of your Swiss I don't think you're going to get the five of us across the frontier back into Germany without a lot of awkward questions being asked.'

Pannwitz was not disconcerted by Cain's

vehemence. 'Yes, I have been giving some thought to that problem myself, and I realize now that you men know as much as the girl about the source of the leak in our High Command, or wherever else it is. Now if you would agree to accompany me back to Germany – we shall fix you up with the necessary documents – I am prepared to let the girl stay behind in Switzerland. We will have no further use for her then.'

'You cold-blooded bastard,' Cain spat out, his mind racing, weighing up the possibilities at a tremendous speed. Pannwitz would have no compunction about handing them over to the Swiss police and he doubted that even the SIS could help them, once they had been sentenced by a Swiss court. On the other hand, they would break soon enough, even the toughest of them, once the Gestapo began working on them in the cellars of Number Ten, Prinz Albrecht Strasse. They were caught between the devil and the deep blue sea!

Abel looked from Pannwitz to Cain, his face white with strain. 'Cain,' he blurted out, 'it's the only way. I'm prepared to go. We all must. My God, don't you realize – she's a Jewess...'

The words died away on his lips. He could see that no one was listening to him. All of them – Pannwitz, Deutscherli, the girl, the Ultra men – were frozen into immobility like actors at the end of a cheap melodrama, waiting for the fall of the curtain. Pannwitz stood there with his back to the big window, his legs astride, hands on hips, a faint knowing smile on his thick lips, complete master of the situation. At his desk, Deutscherli, his face full of pride, his hand on his pistol, was ready to shoot, hoping that the white-faced Englishmen *would* move so that he could mow them down like the racially inferior scum they were. And the girl! Abel wondered what must be going on in her mind at this terrible moment.

At that moment, Rosamund Hirsch really hated someone for the first time in her life. Before, her hatred of the swaggering storm troopers who had pushed her off the pavement as soon as they had seen the yellow star of the Jew, the officers who had fumbled her breasts and had tried to work their knees between her legs in countless provincial theatres, the whip-cracking, black-uniformed guards in the Camp, had been quickly submerged by fear, by a desire to please, to submit – anything to avoid punishment. Not now!

Now she was possessed by a burning, overwhelming hatred of the man who stood poised in front of the window, arrogant, all-powerful, all-knowing: the living symbol of the oppression, the great wrong committed against her and her kind all these last terrible years. She was no longer afraid. Now she knew only one thing. Pannwitz must never be allowed to win again.

Something snapped within Rosamund Hirsch. The hatred was replaced by a great passionate anger. She threw her head back wildly. She stretched her mouth in one high passionate shriek. Before anyone could stop her, she rushed forward at the arrogant Gestapo man, and crashed into him.

Pannwitz was caught completely off guard. Desperately he tried to regain his balance. His hands clutched and caught Rosamund Hirsch's dress. But there was no stopping her crazed rush. Pannwitz's face contorted with fear. '*Nein–*' he screamed hysterically. There was the crash of breaking glass. The next moment the two of them had vanished through the big picture window, trailing a wild, long-drawn scream behind them.

Mac was the first to break that awesome, loud-echoing silence. He cried something in Gaelic and lashed out with his big ham of a fist.

Deutscherli shot up from his chair and slammed against the wall. He groaned once, his eyes rolling upwards to reveal the whites. Slowly he began to slither down the wall, blood trickling from his nostrils, to slump in an untidy, unconscious heap on the floor.

'For God's sake – quick!' Abel yelled. Suddenly galvanised into action, he rushed to the shattered window. He craned his neck out and then gasped, shocked.

Cain thrust him to one side and he leaned groggily against the wall, his handsome young face bloodless, the colour of clay. Cain looked down. Dark little figures were streaming in from all sides towards the spot where the two of them – the Jewess and the Gestapo-man – lay in the dirty snow. But there nothing moved, saved the thin trickle of red blood spreading ever outwards. They were dead, those bitter enemies, clasped in each other's arms, like two lovers.

He turned and shook his head wearily.

'Oh my God,' Abel gasped. *'Oh my God!'*

And then the four of them were clattering wildly down the stairs of the Customs Headquarters. A bespectacled customs official tried to bar the way. Spiv kneed him. He went down, choking in his own vomit. The receptionist who had put them in the lift, grabbed for his pistol. Cain's hook hissed through the air. The man screamed with agony, staggering back as bright red blood spurted through the fingers tightly clutched to his injured hand. They burst through the door.

Outside, a thick crowd had gathered around Pannwitz and the dead girl, staring at the still bodies and pointing upwards at the shattered windows. The Ultra men burst through them, scattering them to left and right. Abel flung himself down beside the girl.

He could guess that most of the bones in her body had been shattered, but her face was perfect, undistorted by fear or any other emotion. She might well have been deep in a dreamless sleep. Gently he pressed his lips against hers, in farewell.

Behind them they could already hear the shrill call of the police whistles and the hoarse cries of rage, as the police discovered what had happened in the Customs HQ. There was no more time to be lost.

'*Halt! Stehenbleiben oder ich schiesse!*' an angry, official voice behind them commanded.

But the policeman was already too late. Zig-zagging crazily, pushing aside the confused civilians, the Ultra men had already disappeared into the maze of streets that made up Schaffhausen's city centre. They were gone for good...

EPILOGUE

'My experience is that the gentlemen who are the best behaved and the most sleek are those who are doing the mischief. We cannot be too sure of anybody.'

Field-Marshal Ironside.

'*Platoon*, platoon – eyes right!'

The skinny second-lieutenant's thin voice was almost drowned by the clatter of an engine shunting over at Paddington Station. But the file of marching men, laden down with full Field Service Marching Order and weapons, responded well enough. As the boy raised his brown-leather gloved hand to his cap, their heads clicked right and their eyes met Cain's. Automatically he touched his hook to his cap, reflecting that they looked like cannon-fodder already.

'*Platoon*, eyes front!'

The platoon stamped away towards the train, which would bear them away to their own particular date with destiny, and Cain turned into the square, located between the Edgware Road and Harrow Road.

Once, the Edwardian houses it contained had been painted and bright, their high steps immaculately kept, their brass door knockers polished to a high gloss, with prim housemaids and proper governesses coming and going down the swept pavements. But that had been long before. Now the railing had been taken away by the Council for the war effort, and the little squares of front gardens were heaped with the rubbish of the last three years – broken shoes, abandoned mattresses, a cracked sink, an old iron bath, too heavy to be lifted by the council workers.

Cain sighed and stared at the buildings, looking for the number he sought. To him, the grimy, rundown houses seemed to symbolize the England of 1943: it too was run down and shabby, kept going only by a sheer effort of will.

Number 22 – the one he sought. Slowly he mounted the steps, narrowly missing the dog excrement with which it was littered and ran his eyes along the little name plates. *Miss Coates, French Lessons By Appointment Only; R. A. Singh, BA (Hons) Bombay; Fred and Joe* – and then he spotted it – *Bletchley!*

'*Bletchley!*' he said under his breath and pressed the bell. How typical of the spymasters to indulge in such puerile humour in the choice of a name for their London safe house! A moment later the door creaked open. A bent, bespectacled woman stood there, black shawl draped over her skinny shoulders: a woman who looked like everybody's granny save for the butt of the small .38 revolver protruding from the shawl.

'Yes?' she quavered, the plates of her overlarge false teeth bulging from her narrow mouth.

'My name's Cain – Major Cain,' he snapped, irritated at having to go through with such foolishness. Sometimes Zero C's attempt at security went a little too far. 'I believe I'm expected.'

The old crone smiled at him. It was a difficult smile, as if her muscles rebelled against the effort. 'Yessir, this way.'

Obediently Cain waited till she had closed – and this time locked – the door, and then followed her slow, creaking progress up the squeaking staircase, scrawled with the graffiti of generations of vandals. She paused at the head of the stairs clasping her skinny claw to her side, as if she had a stitch, but Cain realized she was just assuring herself that her pistol was still there. 'Third door on the right, sir,' she said and plumping herself on the chair, by the landing wall, she pulled an old grey army sock out of her pocket, and began fumbling a darn with arthritic fingers.

Cain shook his head in wonder and crossing to the door, knocked. It was opened at once, as if Zero C had been listening behind it all the time.

'Good to see you again, Cain,' he exclaimed with surprising energy for him. 'Come right in.' As the door closed behind Cain, someone switched on a radio further up the corridor, and again Cain was regaled with the Beverley Sisters' newest opus:

'Well, dig, dig, well alright
Chop, chop, well alright

257

The music'll sock it you.
You know tonight's the night.'

Cain sighed, a pained look on his lean, bronzed face, and Zero C said apologetically, 'Security, you know.'

'I know,' Cain answered wearily.

The tall grey spymaster indicated the man standing next to the fire which glowed solid orange, although it was a warm July night. 'You know C of course, Cain?'

Cain nodded, surprised to see the product of Eton, the Life Guards, and White's, in such a dump standing in front of the woollen underwear and black socks hanging to dry on the high brass fireguard. But still, he knew, that it had been C, the head of the Secret Intelligence Service, who had first started this system of 'safe houses' throughout the United Kingdom.

He saluted and C offered his hand. As Cain took it he was aware of C's cold, dead eyes sizing him up; eyes that had seen many men sent to their deaths, with indifference.

Zero C looked at Cain keenly, taking in the emaciated, brown face, the dark shadows under the eyes and the tense compressed lips. 'Well, we pulled it off, Cain, eh?' he said with forced cheerfulness.

'Yes, *we* did, sir.' The irony was wasted on the spymasters.

'You fit, Cain?' C snapped.

'Yessir.'

'Good.' He nodded to his subordinate Zero C.

'Well, perhaps since you came back, you have had a chance to have a look at the papers, Cain,' Zero C continued. 'You've seen that the Boche have really been given a bloody nose at Kursk. They'll never be able to field another army like the one they lost in Central Russia – thanks to Bletchley, eh?' Cain nodded. He had read the papers. The Germans were on the retreat everywhere. Their spring-summer offensive had been a complete failure.

'And the Rado Ring, sir?' Cain asked.

'They have served their purpose,' C answered the question. 'We passed the tip about them to the BUPO ourselves. Punter is already in custody. Rado,' he chuckled suddenly for some reason known only to himself, 'has applied for asylum to the British Embassy, which fortunately will have ruined him completely with Moscow. The Swiss will pick him up soon.'

'And the spy of the century, sir?' Cain asked.

'Lucy? Oh, he's already been picked up. One wonders what the writer chappies will make of his testimony to the Swiss police, when they get their greedy little hands on it after the war?' Zero C said, obviously pleased with the thought. 'Such a collection

259

of banal trivialities!'

Cain did not react. Suddenly he realized just what a pawn he – and the hundreds of other agents employed by the SIS – were in the hands of such men as C and Zero C. The spymasters allowed them, the pawns, to believe that they were important, had an independence of action, could make decisions and act and react any way they liked. But in reality, they were just pieces on a gigantic chessboard to be used and dispensed with when the men in the shadows felt they had outlived their usefulness. 'And Jim?' he asked finally.

'Yes, Cain, that is why we called you here this evening.' At a nod from C, his assistant walked to the other door and opened it.

Jim walked in, hand extended, lazy cynical grin on his face as usual. 'Cain, good to see you again!' he exclaimed happily.

'How did you get out?'

'Not by being on the run in the Jura like you chaps for two months, though I must say it gave you a very nice tan. Must go down well with the ladies. No, I came out by the weekly Madrid plane, Lisbon, the Clipper and all that, you know?'

Cain knew, but he wondered how Jim had avoided being picked up by the *Bupo*. Surely Lucy would have talked? Or Punter? But Cain had little time to consider the problem, for suddenly C said, 'It's important for our plan–'

'Plan?' Cain cut in.

'Nothing you need to know about, Cain. As I was saying it is important for us to know if anyone else was aware of your association with Jim here.'

'The Swiss policeman, Muessli, Pannwitz and the–' Cain hesitated for a moment – 'German woman knew of it. But they are all dead. Why do you ask, sir?'

'Nothing you need to know about, Cain. In our business it is wise not to let the right hand know what the left one is doing. I'm sure you understand that,' he added grimly.

'Yessir.'

'Good. Bear it in mind. So there is no way that anyone can associate you with Jim. Excellent.' He looked at the radio operator, whose face had become unusually serious for him. 'It's on then.'

'I suppose so, sir.' Jim answered slowly.

But C, the head of the Secret Intelligence Service, had no time for procrastination now. Suddenly he seemed in a great hurry. 'All right, Cain, this is the situation. Jim will be going down to Southampton tomorrow night. The arrangements have already been made and false identity papers have been issued. Now this is going to be Ultra's role…'

Cain walked out in a daze. Vaguely he realized that the spymasters were already beginning to feel out the new enemy; exactly how and why he did not know. But around that 18th century table behind the green baize door on the second floor of the neat little house in Queen Anne's Road, they had already hatched new plans, because it smelt right to do so, and fitted into their cynical, conspiratorial way of thinking. This war was not yet over – though it was clearly won – and already they were preparing to meet the new enemy in the shadows.

The rest of the Ultra team were waiting for him at Paddington Station Salvation Army's canteen for the Armed Forces among the comings and goings of servicemen bearing their jam-jars of tea – 'can't trust you soldiers with cups, you break too many of them!' – and plates of beans on toast.

The seven days' leave had done them a world of good, but they were all still a good ten pounds under their normal weight. When a young able-seaman dropped his jam-jar of tea to the accompaniment of stamping feet and whistles from the packed canteen, all of them started nervously, even the dour Scot Mac.

Spiv, who was liberally dousing his tea with Scotch from a flask, in spite of the severe tut-tutting of one of the bonneted assistants, spotted him first. 'Over here, sir,' he yelled above the racket. 'Make way for a naval officer there!'

Cain cursed under his breath and striding over to them rapped, 'Outside! I want to talk to you. We've got a rush job.'

'Knackers!' Spiv said, his drunken grin vanishing abruptly, 'I haven't even had time to dip me wick in proper yet. This ruddy war is really interfering with my love life, I can tell yer that. I shouldn't be surprised if it doesn't drop off from lack of use any day now.'

'Ay, pity the same thing didn't happen to yon tongue of yours,' Mac growled, rising to his feet. 'But the way ye blabber on, that'll never happen, I'm afeared.'

Obediently they followed him on to the crowded platform, pushing their way through the shabby civilians and the heavily laden servicemen.

The big old-fashioned gas lamps were beginning to go on now, bathing the faces of the crowd in their yellow hissing light, turning them into anxious ghosts, shadow-faced with dead lips.

'We've all been given gongs,' Cain announced when they had reached the end of the long platform and could not be over-heard.

'Not the VC?' Spiv queried, remembering his great days as Colonel Hake-Smythe.

'Nothing so grand! DSO for me, MC for

263

Mr Abel and Mac here–'

'I know,' Spiv interrupted him, 'the sodding Military Medal for me. I've got a chestful of the buggers already. We workers allus get the dirty end of the stick.' He pulled out his flask and took a slug of his whisky. 'I sometimes wonder why I help you blokes, the way I do.'

The three of them grinned; Spiv was in his usual form.

'And the mission, skipper?' Abel asked, the old happy light gone from his eyes now, burdened as his memory was for ever with Rosamund Hirsch's death.

Cain pursed his lips. Across the way, the guard was raising his green flag and there was a frantic last minute slamming of doors and calling of best wishes. 'You're not going to like it. But you are all going to Switzerland again.'

'*What?*' they exclaimed in astonished unison.

''Fraid so. I can't tell you much. But we've been ordered to protect Jim – you know about him? – until he is arrested by the Swiss police. Don't ask me why. But we'll get new ID, so we've nothing to worry about. It'll be a routine mission…'

On the other platform the guard blew his whistle shrilly. The great heavy engine shuddered. Slowly it began to draw away, followed by the anxious cries of those who would remain behind – the despairing commonplaces of wartime partings – 'Write soon, father … look after yourself, son … hurry back soon, darling … never forget me, will you?…'

Again the engine shuddered violently, its gleaming wheels seeming to slip on the rails. A great cloud of grey steam shot out from its side and ascended to the shattered glass roof, blotting out the platform.

'Oh, Christ on a crutch,' a thin cockney voice protested above the noise, *'not ferking Switzerland agen!'*

Then there was the hollow sound of heavy, steel-tipped boots hurrying down the wet, trash-littered platform. A moment later the smoke had vanished and the platform was empty.

ULTRA WAS GOING TO WAR AGAIN…

AUTHOR'S NOTE

For those who are interested in historical mysteries, there has never been any explanation offered – officially or unofficially – for Alexander Foote's (alias 'Jim') mission back to Switzerland. In due course, he was arrested, sentenced and released once the Swiss were sure the Allies were going to win the war. In April 1945, he and Rado were flown to Moscow in General Eisenhower's personal plane – the first direct flight from Paris to Moscow since 1939.

At a stopover Rado, it is said, tried to defect. Without success. As 'C' had confidently predicted at the Paddington safe house two years before, Rado had compromised himself by attempting to seek refuge at the British Embassy in Berne. In Moscow he was taken to the notorious Llubjanka Jail, interrogated – and presumably tortured – before being sentenced to ten years' imprisonment.

Foote, on the other hand, was awarded another Soviet decoration and according to his own statements, given some specialist training in a Russian Intelligence school.

In 1946 he returned to East Berlin as a captain in the Red Army. What his mission was thereon in Moscow has never been established. In the summer of that year he 'defected' and was returned to Britain. Naturally no charges were ever pressed against the 'renegade' and one-time 'Soviet agent', although by now the Cold War had started in earnest.

Instead, he was quietly moved into the calm backwater of London's Ministry of Agriculture and Fishery, where he was employed as a minor clerk. And there he died in the depths of the old 'Min. of Ag. And Fish' in the mid-fifties, bearing the secret of his last mission with him to the grave.

The publishers hope that this book has given you enjoyable reading. Large Print Books are especially designed to be as easy to see and hold as possible. If you wish a complete list of our books please ask at your local library or write directly to:

Magna Large Print Books
Magna House, Long Preston,
Skipton, North Yorkshire.
BD23 4ND

This Large Print Book, for people
who cannot read normal print,
is published under the auspices of

THE ULVERSCROFT FOUNDATION